PEP TALKS

Pepper Jones #4

ALI DEAN

COPYRIGHT

Copyright © 2015 Ali Dean.

Edited by Leanne Rabessa at Editing Juggernaut
Cover design by Hang Le

All rights reserved. This book or any portion thereof may not be reproduced or used in any manner whatsoever without the express written permission of the publisher except for the use of brief quotations in a book review.

This is a work of fiction. Names, characters, places, and incidents either are the product of the author's imagination or, if an actual place, are used fictitiously and any resemblance to actual persons, living or dead, business establishments, events, or locales is entirely coincidental.

This book may not be re-sold or given away to other people. If you would like to share this book with another person, please purchase an additional copy for each person you share it with. If you are reading this book and did not purchase it, or it was not purchased for your use only, then you should return it to the seller and purchased your own copy. Libraries are exempt and permitted to share their in-house copies with their member and have full thanks for stocking this book. Thank you for respecting the author's work.

❦ Created with Vellum

CHAPTER ONE

"Dude, if you finish everything on your tray, I'll be super impressed," Lexi tells me as we settle around a large circular table with the rest of our cross country teammates. "Or totally freaked out. I haven't decided yet."

It's my first meal at Chapman Hall, the cafeteria at University of Colorado at Brockton reserved for athletes only. And there were simply too many choices for dinner; I couldn't decide. So I've chosen some of just about everything. My tray must weigh at least ten pounds.

"Let the girl fuel up, we've got triple workouts tomorrow," Kiki Graves says. She's co-captain of the cross team along with Sienna Darling, who hosted me for my recruit trip last fall.

"No worries, guys, you won't have to roll me outta here. I'm just going to take a little sample of everything," I explain with a shrug.

"That's wasteful," Gina points out. She's one of my three roommates and I got the impression that she dislikes me from the moment I met her. Well, I guess we met during my recruit trip last year, but I don't remember her being cold then. Since arriving at the dorm suite early this morning to move in, she hasn't been especially friendly. I haven't decided if that's just her personality, or if there's something special about me.

"I won't make it a habit, Gina." She does make a decent point. "Promise."

Gina scowls before returning to her salad. Lexi raises her eyebrows and glances at me in question. Like, what did you do to piss her off? Shrugging, I decide to dig into the roast beef first, and discover it's dry as sandpaper.

Lexi giggles at my expression. "I should've warned you to stay away from the meat dishes." Lexi Morris is a California girl, through and through. Her blonde curly hair is barely contained by a ponytail and she's rocking a deep summer tan with a spattering of freckles over her nose and cheeks to top it off. We hit it off at the recruit trip last fall and I was beyond thrilled to learn she'd be one of my roommates this year. Gina and Lexi are sophomores, but our fourth roommate is a freshman like me.

I haven't gotten a good read on Caroline Hopkins yet. She's the last one to join the table. There are twelve of us seated around the large circular table, and I suppose we'll have to divide the team over two tables when the rest of them arrive. There are eighteen total on the roster this year, and the remaining six won't get here until tomorrow.

"Ladies, what's this all about?" a guy asks as he hovers by our table with a tray. "You didn't save us any seats?"

"Go away, Brax." Kiki flicks her hand in a shooing gesture. "Girls only at this table tonight. We're *bonding*," she says dryly.

"Where are we supposed to sit?" Brax asks.

Kiki tilts her head, refusing to respond to the question, given that there are plenty of open tables.

Another guy throws an arm around Brax. "There will be plenty of opportunities to flirt with the girls later, man," he says before steering him to the table where the men's team is sitting. Brax winks at Lexi as he passes, and she rolls her eyes.

"He's the ultimate flirt," she explains.

I've heard of Brax Hilton. He's a junior, and a top runner on the team. I've never met him before, though, and I certainly don't know anything about his flirting habits.

Sienna glances at me and the other four freshmen at the table:

Caroline, Wren Jackson, Erin Tokac, and Kendra Smith. Kendra is the only other freshman from Colorado, and we raced each other a few times in high school. "We usually sit with the guys' team after practice," Sienna explains. "I don't know what it was like for all of you in high school, but at UC, the men's and women's teams are pretty close. Sure, we compete separately, but we have the same coach and we support each other."

I nod along with the other freshmen. It was like that at Brockton Public. While the excitement of my new teammates has provided a welcome distraction, there's definitely an ache in my chest for my old teammates. Zoe, Rollie, Omar, Jenny... they were my best friends. I know they will always be my friends, but it won't be the same. Zoe left yesterday for Mountain West, two hours away from UC at Brockton. Omar is going to State, which is even farther away in the southwestern corner of the state. And Rollie is going to college in Boston. Jenny is still in Brockton, and it's hard to believe she's a junior, an *upperclassman*, and co-captain of the Brockton Public cross team. It seems like yesterday she was only a freshman.

Our goodbye party a couple of days ago involved too much alcohol and tears. Jenny and Rollie started dating months ago, and they are going to try the long-distance thing. Zoe and one of my childhood friends, Wesley Jamison, casually dated for months before Wes left for Princeton last week. Wes never had a girlfriend before Zoe, but I don't think either of them considered it anything serious, despite how long it lasted. We all knew Wes would be heading to Princeton after his deferral year was up.

I'm the lucky one in love, I guess. My boyfriend, Jace Wilder, is a sophomore at UC, and he lives within walking distance. After spending his freshman year in the dorms (which is mandatory), he decided to move off-campus with his teammate Frankie Zimmer.

As though my thoughts have conjured the man himself, I watch Jace Wilder enter Chapman Hall surrounded by an entourage of gigantic football players. In high school, Jace's six-foot-three frame of solid muscle was a dominating presence, and he's gotten even stronger and his muscles even bigger since starting college a year ago. His size isn't especially outstanding compared to his teammates', but when he breaks away and heads toward our table after catching my eye, it's hard not to gawk. He's twice the size of most girls on my team.

Jace ignores the eleven sets of eyes from the other females at my table as he crouches behind me and kisses me on the cheek in greeting. I turn to face him, and he's giving me a panty-dropping smile. I'm determined not to be the freshman girl who peaces out all the time to be with her boyfriend, but when he flashes me a grin like this, I'm really tempted to ditch my lonely dorm room tonight for his king-size bed off campus.

"How's the first day going?" he asks quietly.

"You saw me several hours ago, Jace." I pretend to be annoyed by his attentiveness, but it's cute. He's so excited for me to be a college student and he wants me to be happy. "But the first run with my team after you left my dorm room was lovely," I appease him.

"Should I introduce myself now?" he asks. He almost sounds tentative, and it's adorable on him. He is an extremely confident young man. And it's not a false confidence either. It's what makes him such a good quarterback. It's how he led UC to the championship finals as a freshman after the team hadn't even made the playoffs for years.

Before I can pipe up, Lexi, who is sitting beside me, eagerly replies, "Hi Jace Wilder, I'm Lexi Morris, Pepper's roommate." She waves and I frown at her.

"Hi Lexi, we already met this morning at the dorm," Jace reminds her, amusement in his voice.

She shrugs. "I know, dude, but I wanted to make sure you remembered my name. It's easy to forget the first time around, and me and your girl are gonna be friends so you should most definitely know who I am."

As Jace introduces himself to the rest of the table, I get the impression that everyone, even a couple of the freshmen, know who he is already. No one seems particularly shocked that he introduces himself as my boyfriend. It's old news by now that Jace Wilder is taken, and given how much time I've spent with Jace on campus over the past year, it's no secret that I'm the lucky girl. And I do feel lucky.

The attention from college girls dwindled when they realized Jace was more interested in football than partying. Though the media didn't catch wind of all the details behind a catastrophic series of incidents with a girl on the UC soccer team who was obsessed with Jace, there was plenty of gossip around campus. It seems most girls did not want to be called a "Savannah Hawkins" – the girl who attacked me in the name of her so-called love for my boyfriend – and decided to let go of any hope of stealing him away from me. So, in one regard, Savannah did me a favor. I guess. I try to think positively.

Jace finally leaves the table, after introducing himself to every single girl, and I can't help but notice the glazed look in my teammates' eyes as they watch him join the football team at the food stations. I don't blame them.

When Sienna blurts, "Hot damn, Pepper, your boyfriend is dreamy," I can't suppress my laughter. Sienna has demonstrated a reserved and serious attitude up until now, and those words coming out of her mouth make me crack up. The rest of the girls join me in laughter, but agree with Sienna's assessment.

"Right on, Sienna," Kiki nods emphatically.

"I'd never seen him up close before," Trish Getty, a junior, gushes.

"Well, we can expect to see a lot of that sexy man with our girl Pepper around, so you ladies better learn to keep your tongues in your mouths," Lexi states.

I dig into the veggie lasagna on my plate, which isn't bad but can't compare to my gran's cooking. I've actually gotten used to the effect Jace has on people – women in particular. My friends in high school had the same reaction to him for a long time, and it didn't entirely dissipate as they got to know him better, but it became manageable. It's taken time, but I've learned to deal with his celebrity status in Brockton and on campus. For a while there, I never thought I'd get used to it, but it rolls off me pretty easily now.

Part of it is that I've become confident in who I am. I no longer wonder why Jace picked me, or what others think about our relationship. I know I'm good for him. I make him better, and he brings out a strength in me I didn't know existed. He helps me find a courage and determination that only comes from unconditional love and understanding. We've been through a lot together, and we've made it.

Against all odds, I won high school cross country nationals last year for the second year in a row. And I don't know if I could have done that if I hadn't built the confidence and strength that's required to be Jace's girlfriend. Uncertainty, weakness, self-doubt – these things can't accompany someone like Jace. He attracts a lot of attention, and it's not always good attention. I had to learn to deal with it. And I have. It's made me a better runner, and maybe a better person.

"You are so totally smitten, girl." Lexi leans in to tease me, and I know I've got the dreamy look in my eyes that I just witnessed on my teammates.

"I'm not denying it." I shrug before moving on to the next entrée – chicken enchiladas.

An hour later, the team is still lounging around the table, though none of us are eating anymore. Some have a cup of coffee or tea, but we're mostly just hanging out to chat and get to know each other. The other teams in Chapman Hall seem to have the same idea, and I wonder if lingering around like this after a meal is common. It's the first day of preseason, so maybe it's an exception. I hope not. I like it. It's nice getting to know the girls for their personalities instead of their running times.

Kiki is definitely the leader. At least, she's the more overt leader. Sienna is quiet, but her presence is a strong one. Gina, I discover, is simply a grumpy person. She isn't all that nice to anyone, which actually makes me feel better that I haven't been singled out. Trish and Lexi entertain us with their banter, and I'm reminded they were roommates last year. Caroline doesn't utter a word throughout the meal, but I can tell she's listening attentively by the way she watches everyone and smiles at the jokes. I'm curious about her, and resolve to get to know her better.

By the time we get back to the dorms and shower, I'm too exhausted to think about anything but crawling into bed. I'm grateful that my bed is in its own room. Though I have three roommates, it's a four-bedroom suite – a great layout that is only afforded to varsity athletes. Until this moment, I hadn't realized what a perk it is be able to go to sleep when I want to, a luxury other freshmen won't have in their double or triple dorm rooms.

It's been a day filled with new experiences, and it's taken all my energy to process. Still, adrenaline runs through me when I turn off the lights and close my eyes. We had an easy group run today, nothing major. But tomorrow is our first real workout, and I'm filled with anticipation.

CHAPTER TWO

Coach Harding is just as friendly in coach-mode as he is in father-mode. The UC head cross coach is Ryan Harding's dad, and Ryan Harding was my first boyfriend during cross season my junior year of high school. Coach Harding welcomed us yesterday, but this morning he gives a more formal speech stating the team goals for the season.

For the women – qualify as a team for Nationals. For the men – top three at Nationals.

The women just missed qualifying as a team last year, though they sent Sienna Darling and a senior who graduated to compete individually. The others didn't race well enough at Regionals to qualify the entire team, but they only missed by one spot.

Seven runners get to compete at Regionals. Two of our top seven graduated last year, but Coach is confident that with the incoming freshman class and recoveries from injuries, we will be even stronger than last year. Lexi was out with an injury last year, so she's considered a "redshirt freshman." She admitted to me that she spent more time surfing than running this summer, but insisted it was only because she didn't want to reinjure herself. I'm not convinced she meant it though.

With Coach Harding's pep talk in mind, and the motivation to not only get the team qualified for Nationals, but to race fast enough to be one of the seven girls who gets to go, we're all fired up for the very first workout. Running practices break down into a few categories: easy/recovery runs, long runs, and "workouts." Within a workout, there are a lot of subcategories – track, tempo, speed, hills, and various types of intervals. Today, we're doing an eight-mile tempo run.

When Coach Harding announces the workout, I wonder for a moment if I had misheard. Did he seriously say eight miles? Eight miles is a long run for me. Long runs are meant to be done at an easy pace. Tempo runs are at a fast pace. Not a full-out sprint, as it's over a few miles, but still faster than comfortable. I've never done a tempo run longer than four miles before.

And then, he tells us the pace we start with on the first mile. My jaw drops and I have to make an effort to shut it. Tempo runs usually get faster as you go. The pace for the first mile of an eight, yes eight, mile run, is generally the pace I end a tempo run with. For the first time in my life, I'm scared of a workout. I actually don't know if I'll make it to the end. I really don't think it's possible for me to continue getting faster each mile, as Coach Harding explains that we should aim to do just that.

We load into large vans to drive to a road where we'll begin the run. The boys are dropped off even farther from campus. They are doing a ten-mile tempo run. Some of the other girls on the team, especially the other freshmen, look nervous, and it makes me feel better that I'm not alone.

All of us stay together for the first few miles, with some of the stronger upperclassmen leading and trading off each mile to set the pace. Coach Harding assigned who would lead each mile until mile six. After that, I guess it's just whoever is still hanging in there.

All of the freshmen have taken positions in the back of the group, because none of us were assigned a mile to lead. Their labored breathing around me at mile four signals that I'm not the only one who's never done an eight-mile tempo run. All five of us were the top runners in our respective high school programs. I'm probably not the only one who is running a workout with girls for the first time in years.

I usually ran with the boys at Brockton Public. As we hit the fifth mile, and the pace picks up again, I realize I might be dropped by girls for the first time ever in workout.

I knew college was a different level, but knowing it and experiencing it are totally different. The team begins to break up during the fifth mile, and I understand why no one was assigned to lead the pace for mile six. Once some of the upperclassmen ahead of us ease up, realizing they can't hold this pace for three more miles, some of the freshmen beside me slow down as well. They didn't want to be the first ones to give up. I'm okay, for now, and I pass those who are slowing down in order to keep up with Trish and Gina, who are setting the pace.

Caroline remains at my side until we hit the last mile. By then, it's only me, Trish, Sienna, and Kiki. In the past, tempo has meant a controlled effort. But right now, I've got to put it all out there to hang with these girls, and I'm pretty sure they are too. It feels like this workout is a test. To see where we all are. Where we stand. And none of us want to back off. We're teammates but right now we're competitors. We're pushing each other, and it's something I've never experienced in practice before. When the three girls leave me in their wake, it's not the same feeling I would have in a race if I was dropped. I'm not losing. In fact, I'm thrilled to have teammates, female teammates, who are faster and stronger than me.

It leaves me with something to work toward. And as soon as they finish, panting and wiped, they gather enough energy to cheer in the rest of the girls on the team. Lexi isn't too far behind, which is impressive for someone who surfed all summer, and Caroline is right with her.

By the time we hit the locker rooms, I remember that Kiki said we had triple workouts today. She must have been mistaken. There's no way we can be expected to run again after that. I'm more wiped than I am after a race.

Thankfully, while we *are* meeting two more times, they aren't nearly as demanding as the morning tempo run. We get a tour of the weight room, but we don't actually lift weights, and then we all go to a yoga class. I'm already familiar with the weight room, since Brockton Public athletes get access to UC facilities, but I've never actually been to a yoga class. My former high school teammate, Claire Padilla, used to have yoga DVDs we'd follow sometimes, but the class is way more intense than what I've done before.

When we hit Chapman Hall for dinner, I'm dead on my feet but excited to see Jace. We haven't made any plans to see each other, and I know he wants me to be able to spend time with the girls on the team. To my dismay, Jace isn't at the cafeteria with the rest of his teammates. I swallow my disappointment and join the cross table. Tonight, the guys' team is intermingled with the girls, and there are three different tables to choose from.

Lexi beckons me to a seat beside her, and I find myself sitting between her and my ex-boyfriend.

"Hey, Ryan." My voice is uncertain. We haven't exchanged even a hello since I joined his team yesterday.

"Hi, Pepper." Ryan's greeting is reserved, not as welcoming as he typically is.

I can tell Lexi is studying us, trying to understand what's going on. She knows that Ryan Harding was my boyfriend at one point. Last fall, after Ryan broke up with his girlfriend at the time, he started spending more time with me. One on one time. Plus, rumors were flying that he broke up with Lisa Delany because he still had feelings for me. Jace didn't like us spending time together. He wasn't a jerk about it, but I knew it wasn't cool for Ryan to be hanging around me like he was, whether or not he wanted more than friendship. When I told Ryan that it was probably best we maintain some space, given I had a boyfriend and he was my ex, he took it to an extreme. He's barely acknowledged my existence since. I don't know what I expected. I suppose I hoped we'd maintain a friendly acquaintance, but I guess that's not so easy.

Now that we're going to be seeing each other again on a regular basis, we need to figure out how it's going to be between us. I don't want to ignore each other. It feels so cold. We aren't enemies and we shouldn't act like it.

"How was your tempo run today?" I ask him. Talking about running is safe.

"Not bad," he responds dismissively. Okay then. So that's how it's going to be.

Brax Hilton pipes in from across the table. "Harding and I battled it out that last mile. You put up a good fight, man," he says, raising his glass, "but you can't take me yet. Maybe someday," he taunts.

Ryan chuckles. "You know I just let you win, Brax. You get all moody when you don't. I didn't want to hurt your feelings."

Guys can tease each other like this but girl teammates can't. Girls are too sensitive, I guess. I envy guys sometimes for how easily things roll off their backs. Of course, guys can be sensitive sometimes too, I'm reminded, as Ryan continues to ignore me throughout dinner.

Lexi tells me, "You know, Coach Harding had us do that same tempo run on the first day last year, and I guess the year before that too."

"Oh, yeah?"

"Yeah, I did it last year before I got injured, and got my ass kicked. Don't worry though, not all of our workouts are that brutal. It's just a chance to gauge where everyone's at going in to the season. You did awesome, dude," she reassures me, punching me lightly on the shoulder. It's what I suspected, then.

"Workouts will be a lot harder than what you were used to at Brockton Public," Ryan adds. Despite acting like he was ignoring me, he was listening to our conversation.

"Oh? Should I be worried?" It sounded like a warning, but Ryan's tone is hard for me to read now. Usually he's so simple and easy to interpret.

"You'll just need to be honest with yourself about what you can handle. You don't want to get injured again." He says all this without looking at me and then returns to his sandwich. Again, I can't tell if he's trying to be nice and helpful, or if he intended that comment as a dig.

I study him for a moment. He's let his hair grow out to nearly chin length, but at the moment, it's pulled back with what appears to be a cut-out shirt sleeve. It's an edgy look. Maybe even a little hipster. He's changed. And not just physically.

Thoughts of Ryan, and how I'm going to deal with him as my teammate, are forgotten when Jace knocks on our dorm suite door later that night. Gina answers, and when I hear his voice I poke my head out of my bedroom door. Gina is stuttering, and the standoffish attitude she's displayed since I met her has dropped. When Jace sees me he grins, and it's all I can do not to drag him into my room and slam the door on my roommates. It's only been a day, but I missed him.

Jace steps around Gina and approaches me. "Are you going to invite me in?" he asks, and I don't miss the intent behind his question.

Glancing briefly behind him, I shoot Gina a small smile and then I do tug him into my bedroom and shut the door behind me.

This is the first time I've had him alone in my new room, and a feisty possessiveness comes over me. I place my hand on his chest and push him back onto my bed. He watches me with hooded eyes and curiosity.

I tap my chin thoughtfully. "I've been waiting all day to get you alone."

"Oh?" Jace is already breathing heavily, and I know he's been waiting all day for this as well.

"Yup." I nod knowingly. "I think you should take this off," I say suggestively, tugging at his cotton tee shirt.

Without a word he pulls it over his head and tosses it aside. Boldly, I slip my hands beneath the waistband of his sweatpants and boxer briefs, and tug the material hard. And just like that, the most beautifully sculpted man is resting sans clothing on my bed.

After a moment watching him, just appreciating the sight, Jace draws my attention back to his face. "I'm starting to feel a little self-conscious here, Pepper," he says.

"You don't look very self-conscious," I reply, my eyes drifting back to the center of his body. "Proud and alert are more accurate adjectives, don't you think?"

With a growl, Jace tugs me onto the bed with him, and it doesn't take long before we've made my new bedroom our own. After spending plenty of time at Jace's dorm last school year, I'm used to staying quiet. No need to make my new roommates uncomfortable. Just knowing Jace is in here with me probably has them in a tizzy already.

Afterward, we lie under the covers, and I'm overwhelmed with a deep exhaustion that is thoroughly satisfying. I love the way my body feels after a hard workout, and with the yoga on top of it, my muscles are beat but loose. With Jace's warm body beside me, I know I'll sleep well. College is looking pretty great so far.

CHAPTER THREE

"Where were you at dinner last night?" I ask groggily the next morning. Jace is shuffling around the room, looking for his clothes. I'd forgotten to ask him this question last night.

"Dinner with Mom," he tells me as he pulls on his sweatpants.

I take a moment to admire his chest and abs before he pulls his tee shirt over his head. The football team is meeting for practice even earlier than the cross team. It's still dark outside, and I'm happy I get to stay in bed another hour.

"How's Annie?" I ask on a yawn. Annie had abandoned Jace when he was a toddler but returned over a year ago. She was young and addicted to drugs when she left, and apparently hasn't touched drugs since she returned. For a long time, I didn't trust her. But she's been a good mom to Jace since she came back, and I don't think he can help loving her.

I know that deep down, Jace always dreamed she'd come back, apologize for leaving, and make up for it. So far, she has done just that.

"She's good. Seeing a guy, actually." Jace's brows furrow when he says this.

"Yeah? Have you met him?"

"I'm supposed to meet him tonight. Do you want to come?"

"Of course," I agree. I'm not keen on missing dinners with the team during preseason, but this is a big deal. Annie hasn't dated anyone since she moved back to Brockton. At least, no one she's told Jace about. It must be pretty serious if she wants to introduce the guy to her son.

"She seems into him," Jace says with a shrug, but I can see through his effort at nonchalance. He's worried. I don't know if that's because he's worried the guy isn't good enough for Annie, or if he's worried she'll stop caring as much about her relationship with her son.

Jace leans over to kiss me goodbye before heading out. Before I can fall back asleep, Lexi pops her head into my room.

"Morning, sunshine," she greets me.

"It's not morning yet, go away," I half-heartedly protest.

"Oh please, I saw your boy leaving just now so I know I didn't wake you." Lexi sits on the edge of my bed.

"So much for going back to sleep," I grumble as I prop myself up on my elbow. "What are you doing up?"

She winks at me. "Woke up early from my sleepover. Wanna grab some breakfast? That way we'll have time to digest before running."

"Wait. Back up. Sleepover?"

"Yeah," she says on a sigh. "Brax Hilton. We messed around a few times last spring and I guess we're doing it again."

"Oh, that's cool. He seems like a good guy," I comment, because I'm not sure how to read the situation. It doesn't sound like she's in love with him, but she did just have a sleepover. I'll never understand casual hookups.

Lexi laughs. "Brax is sweet, and sure, I guess he's a good guy, but he's a total flirt."

"You're okay with that?" I wonder.

"Oh yeah, I knew what he was all about the first time we made out. He's not the kind of guy who's looking for a girlfriend. And to be honest, I'm not looking for a boyfriend either. Freedom and independence in college and all that," she says with a wave of her hand.

"Hey, I feel plenty free and independent with my boyfriend," I point out.

"Puh-lease, you two are a total exception. Anyone who looks at you two can see you're crazy about each other. But most people don't have that, and it's not worth having a serious relationship in college for some lukewarm feelings, you know? I had a boyfriend in high school, so I'm not opposed to the whole monogamy thing. Now's just not the time for it. Unless I find me a Jace Wilder to looooooove," she teases, pushing me lightly on the shoulder so I fall back onto my pillow. "Get dressed, girl, I'm starved."

As I pull on some sweats and sneakers, it dawns on me that Lexi has made herself my new best friend. Because only best friends show up and sit on each other's beds at the crack of dawn, chatting about sleepovers. And I'm okay with that. Lexi reminds me of my other best girlfriend, Zoe. For starters, they both have way too much energy first thing in the morning. A small wave of nostalgia hits me thinking that Zoe is now relegated to my high school bestie, and we'll both have new college besties. She's not being replaced, not exactly, but the loss of seeing her every day still tugs at me. There's a grief and mourning process involved in this college transition that no one warned me about. Sure, I'm still in Brockton, my hometown, but my life is changing rapidly, and I'm leaving the old one behind.

When we load our trays at the cafeteria and head toward the tables I've come to recognize as the cross country team's section, we see Brax, Ryan, and another guy I recognize from the cross team are already there.

"What's up, guys?" Lexi places her tray down, not even looking at Brax. He watches her as he takes a sip of coffee.

"Yo, Pepper Jones, I'm Zeb," the one guy I haven't met puts his hand out and introduces himself.

"Nice to meet you," I say with a smile.

"Heard you rocked the tempo run, well done," Zeb says on a nod.

"Uh, thanks." I'm not used to team gossip about workouts. But I get the feeling the tempo run is an initiation of sorts on the UC team.

"Thanks for the alarm clock at five AM, Lexi," Ryan says with a knowing smirk.

Lexi sputters on her orange juice when his comment sinks in. She glances at Brax, her cheeks reddening. Brax doesn't seem fazed. He just grins and takes another sip of coffee.

"Let's try to keep the moaning under wraps before seven AM going forward, cool?" Ryan adds.

Lexi responds by punching him on the shoulder, and Ryan winces.

Zeb laughs. "I guess the sex noises don't drift down to the first floor. I only got the springs squeaking."

"Oh my gawd." Lexi covers her face with her hands. "No one ever told me the yellow house has paper-thin walls."

Brax turns to me. "The yellow house has been the guys' cross house for years. Eight of us live there."

"Eight cross guys in one house, huh?" I grasp the opportunity to change the subject, because it's probably making me almost as uncomfortable as Lexi. I'm not used to talking about sex so openly like this. "No drama?"

"Drama? Nah, guys don't do drama. A hell of a lot of stinky laundry though," Brax says.

"I can only imagine," I murmur.

If Lexi was trying to keep her fling – or whatever it is – with Brax quiet, she failed. I'm sure the whole cross team, guys and girls, will know by the end of the day.

"So, you guys going to the Sig Beta-Theta Kapp party tonight?" Lexi asks, and we all laugh, knowing she's making an effort to talk about anything other than what goes on at the yellow house.

Brax takes the bait. "You know we'll all be there, Lexi. Officially it's just Theta Kapp hosting, though. You know about what went down with Sig Beta, right?"

We nod. Sigma Beta fraternity was put on probation last year when it was discovered that the president, Gage Fitzgerald, was selling not only steroids, but also a wide variety of recreational drugs. But Gage was only a small piece of a wider corruption problem for Sig Beta. The fraternity was suspended for the entire school year nationwide when an investigation revealed that drug dealing and other illegal activity was taking place in the Sig Beta fraternity on other college campuses, too.

I don't know the whole story, but Gage Fitzgerald's downfall seems to have been the first of a domino effect for Sig Beta.

"Water theme this year. Should be interesting," Brax adds.

"Water theme? What does that even mean?" Lexi asks.

"Slip 'n' slides, hot tubs, bikinis," Zeb says dreamily. "*Lots* of bikinis."

"Don't get too excited, Zebulon," Lexi enunciates his full name, "we all know the Theta Kapp girls go for the big muscular men. No offense, guys," she adds.

"What? I've got guns. And you know I've got a rocking six-pack. Some of the baseball and football dudes are all chub."

As the guys continue to joke about the various teams and athlete body types, I remember hearing about this party last year. Apparently it's tradition for the "hottest" frat and sorority on campus to host a party during preseason for all the athletes on campus. Most varsity athletes don't have time to be part of the Greek system, but the houses want to get the athletes coming to their parties. Maybe Jace and I will make an appearance after dinner with his mom.

As it turns out, both of us can really use the distraction of a party after the dinner. Lance, Annie's boyfriend, is sleazy. We meet at a pizza joint, and he's in a suit, having come straight from work. His hair is slicked back and I notice a fancy watch on his wrist when he shakes our hands. I don't have anything against fancy watches, but the bling on his is a bit much.

Lance spends most of the evening talking about himself, without asking Jace, Annie, or me any questions. He doesn't even try to get to know his girlfriend's son. Lance is a venture capitalist, but I zone out when he launches into a more detailed description of his job. He gives me the creeps and I can't understand why Annie is with him. Annie's pretty easy-going, and dresses in casual, comfortable clothes. She works at the library, and seems content living a simple life. I totally don't see the attraction between these two.

By the time Jace and I are back in his Jeep, we're both tense.

"I'm not going to lie, Jace. Red flags are flying all over the place with that dude." There's no point in denying it. And I want Jace to open up about this. He's gotten a lot better about talking things through instead of burying them, but it usually takes some prompting.

Jace grips the steering wheel and shakes his head. "What the hell is my mom doing with that fucker?" The rage in his voice startles me.

Whoa. "She looks at him like he's some angel, and he's a fucking sleazeball." When Jace slams his hand on the wheel in emphasis, I place a calming hand on his thigh.

"I'm sure Annie will figure that out. She seems like a smart woman."

Jace laughs darkly. "My mom's past tells me she's not the best judge of character."

"What do you mean?" She was a drug addict, but that doesn't reflect on her relationship choices, does it? After all, she was with Jim Wilder, Jace's dad, who's great.

"It was a boyfriend who got her into hard drugs in the first place," Jace says coldly, but I know it's not directed at me. "And it was always boyfriends who kept her from getting sober. She's tired now, from destroying her body all those years, but she was beautiful once. And she looked for love in the wrong places." Jace's assessment doesn't surprise me. There's little doubt his mother was gorgeous. She still is, though she looks older than her years. She must have spoken with Jace about her past, and I don't like that she blamed boyfriends for her drug use.

"Are you going to tell her what you think of Lance?" I ask.

"She'll know without me saying anything that I don't like the guy. If I need to say more, I will. But I can't stop her from seeing the fucker. I'm not her mother. She's mine."

Still, I know this is going to eat at Jace. His relationship with his mom doesn't need any complications. It's complicated enough on its own.

I'd mentioned the party to Jace earlier, telling him I wanted to at least stop in and say hi to my teammates. He didn't seem enthused about going before the dinner, but now he's driving directly to the frat.

I've never been to a frat party as a college student. I showed up at a couple last year with Jace, but I was only there for him then. He'd go briefly to say hello and appease his teammates, who gave him a hard time for rarely going out with them. But now, I have my own teammates at the party, and I wonder how that will play out. Will Jace hang with the cross team? Will I hang with the football players? Will we all hang together?

When both of us are approached and dragged in opposite directions, I'm not given much of an opportunity to contemplate the best approach to the social dynamics. Kiki spots me from across the lawn and beelines in my direction. She's wearing tiny cotton shorts and a string bikini top and carrying a bottle of vodka. I'm not sure what I expected from my team captain, but this wasn't it.

"Pepper! Where have you been?" She doesn't sound accusatory, just perplexed as to my whereabouts. Before I can respond, she's tugging me toward a makeshift bar where jello shots await. When I glance behind me, Jace is already surrounded by people. Oh well, it's probably for the best I hang with my teammates for now anyway. He's extra intimidating when he's in a bad mood and I don't want him scaring off my new friends.

Kiki doesn't pressure me when I decline jello shots, but she does scold me for my lack of appropriate attire. "That's a cute dress, Pepper, but where's your bathing suit?"

Glancing around, I realize I'm the only girl out here not wearing a bikini. I'd considered throwing one in my bag when we left for dinner earlier, just in case, but I didn't think everyone would actually wear bathing suits.

When Lexi approaches, she immediately joins Kiki in scolding me. "We even got Caroline to wear a bikini top!" Lexi beams, apparently proud of her ability to coerce our shy roommate into wearing something outside her comfort zone.

"No worries, my friends," Kiki announces with a flourish. "I came prepared."

I raise my eyebrows at Lexi as Kiki takes my arm and drags me into the frat house. She finds a bag under a pile of clothing and whips out a purple strapless bikini. Shoving it into my hands, she points to the bathroom behind me. "Go, change, we'll wait here."

"Do you have shorts? Most girls out there are wearing shorts."

"Nope. You'll be fine."

With a huff, I take the bathing suit and head into the bathroom. I've got a wicked shorts tan line from all the running I do, but it's dark out so hopefully I won't look too ridiculous.

When I step out of the bathroom, covering myself with my dress self-consciously, Lexi tugs the dress away. "Just pretend you're at the beach or a pool party. There is a makeshift pool thing set up, actually."

"Ew. There's no way I'm getting in that." I probably sound like a snob, but seriously, I know what goes on at these parties and I'm sure there are all kinds of bodily fluids in there.

"Good call, Jones," Kiki says with a nod as she leads us through the house. "Already saw a girl on the soccer team hurl in there."

"Yum."

Lexi giggles. "This is so much fun," she says, throwing an arm around my shoulder. "I love partying with my teammates."

Lexi's a little unsteady on her feet, and when we join the rest of the team on the lawn in the back yard, I discover she's not the only one who's had quite a bit to drink. My friends in high school drank at parties, and it makes sense the same thing would happen in college. But for some reason, I thought my teammates would be too serious about running to drink like other college students. It just doesn't seem possible that these girls can run as fast as they do and still get drunk on the weekends. I suppose I should know better. I mean, I've seen how some of Jace's teammates party, and they're mostly scholarship athletes too.

It makes me wonder if I'm being silly by not drinking. I'm reminded that Jace is the best athlete at UC and he only had a beer or two once in a while. Even during the off season in the spring, when his teammates got drunk on a regular basis, Jace didn't join them. Whoever would have thought Jace Wilder would be my inspiration for sobriety in college? The boy was the center of every party in high school.

A firm arm snakes around my bare waist, and I startle before recognizing the familiar body behind me. "There you are," Jace says in my ear. When I smell alcohol on his breath, I frown and turn in his arms to look at him.

"You're drinking?" I just thought of him as my inspiration, and now he's changing his tune?

"Just one shot with Frankie," he admits. "And this beer." Jace holds up a red solo cup. He actually looks a little guilty, and I feel bad for sounding so accusatory. It wasn't exactly a joyful dinner before we arrived here.

"Sorry, I was just surprised. You don't drink much anymore."

"I just thought I'd take the edge off after listening to Lance the fucker for an hour."

I laugh. "Are you ever going to be able to say his name without a curse involved?"

"No," he says darkly.

We both seem to notice simultaneously that the commotion from a slip 'n' slide competition has dwindled, and instead people are watching us. I blame Jace having taken his shirt off. Sure, every other guy here is shirtless and some are actually wearing Speedos, but my boyfriend's chest truly is quite remarkable. Jace, however, blames *my* bathing suit.

"Pepper, what the hell are you wearing?" He pulls back to glance at me, and I wonder how he missed my lack of clothing when he first approached.

I roll my eyes. "Kiki made me. Blame her!" I point in Kiki's direction, and she's looking our way. She grins back with an innocent little wave, undaunted by Jace's glare.

"This is not appropriate for a frat party," he says so earnestly, I can't help the tug of a smile on my lips.

"Jace, baby, look around. Every girl here is wearing the same thing." My voice is sweet and a little patronizing. He can get so "roar" about other guys looking at me, it's cute.

He doesn't look around, he just pulls me to him, like he can hide my body with his. "Maybe, but you attract more attention than any of them." With a shudder, he whispers, "I can practically feel the vultures circling. I'm not leaving your fucking side unless you put more clothes on." I think he's partially kidding, but I don't mind his possessiveness. I'm not keen on being approached by drunk guys looking for a hookup anyway. Vultures lurking or not, I'm just happy with Jace Wilder at my side.

CHAPTER FOUR

Jace

Pepper's warm body tucked under my arm keeps me calm. We split up when we got to this party, and my anxiety level skyrocketed. My brain is stuck on my mom's boyfriend. I don't want him in our lives. I'm really tempted to break that shit up. He's not good for my mom, yet she's into him. The fucker has charmed her somehow. He's got the kind of face some girls like and he's in decent shape. The jerk might have some money – at least, he acts like he does – but my mom didn't strike me as someone so shallow. It really pisses me off. What is she thinking? Was she with loser druggies for so long that she thinks that's all she deserves?

My blood was starting to boil and I took a shot with the guys. I can't even remember the last time I did that, but my teammates were amped to keep it going with me and that's when I knew I needed Pepper. She brings me out of the dark when it's threatening to suck me under.

I'm trying real hard to give her enough space to do her thing. She's a freshman, and she doesn't need me shadowing her as she makes new friends and figures out college life. But shit, my mom's boyfriend has me ready to hit something, and I know I can't go there. It's her life. If we had a more normal mother-son relationship I might get in the middle of her love life, but I'm afraid she'll chose him over me if I try to interfere. My thoughts are my enemy right now, and that's why Pepper's going to have to stay glued to my side.

The expansive lawn is littered with girls showing off their summer tans. Some of them barely have their boobs covered, but the female skin assaulting my vision doesn't affect me. The only body I'm interested in is safely in my arms as we take in the scene around us.

I've been paying attention to the UC cross team since I was a freshman. I knew Pepper would be on the team, and these people will be her scene. The men's and women's teams are close, which I actually like because it means they watch out for each other and keep to themselves more than some of the other athletes. The girls don't seem bitchy, though a couple of them sleep around. I've heard Trish's name come up amongst the guys a few times. I'm not worried. The cross team's probably the best social group to look out for her, and I'm relieved she's not joining a team full of drama queens or fuck-ups. There are more than a few like that.

Pepper tilts her head up to look at me. "The slip 'n' slide is calling my name," she admits with a grin.

She looks so damn excited.

"Is it, now?"

Pepper picks up on the mischief in my voice and she narrows her eyes suspiciously. Then, without warning, she ducks out from under my arm and sprints away. Instantly, I feel the loss of her body pressed next to mine, but I quickly recover from the shock and chase after her. The girl can run, no doubt about it, but she doesn't have my speed.

I catch her just as she dives onto the slip 'n' slide, head first. I've forgotten to toss my beer, and the red solo cup is still in one hand as my other arm snakes around her. We rush downhill together, my body covering hers as she squeals, uninhibited and totally wrapped up in the moment, in me. Not wanting to crush her I roll onto my back, taking her with me, and our momentum slows when we hit the grass, though it's slick from hose water running down all night, and we glide a little farther before coming to a halt.

Beer from my cup has spilled all over Pepper's chest, and it takes some willpower not to kiss and lick it off. There are gawkers taking this in, and I'm all too aware that Pepper Jones in a bikini is a powerful image. I'm not about to let her star in anyone's visual fantasies but mine.

I revel in Pepper's laughter before pulling her up to her feet with me, and limit myself to a kiss on her shoulder before wrapping my arm protectively around her waist.

She feels so good right here with me, her wet skin sliding against mine as we walk back up the hill. A lot more people are out back now, and it seems my teammates have made their way from the front lawn too. I'm used to eyes following me, and I'm proud to show everyone that yeah, we are a fucking perfect couple. We fit together. We look right together. We *feel* right together. She makes me happy, brings me a peace I can't find anywhere else. Not by working out, playing football, or drinking with the guys. With Pepper at my side, my mom's boyfriend doesn't mean shit to me.

CHAPTER FIVE

After a couple of weeks of preseason with just the athletes on campus, the rest of the students show up, and there's an energy in the air I've never experienced before. When I walk between lecture halls on my first day of college classes, it's overwhelming how many new faces there are. It's a relief I've already made friends and established myself on the cross team. Because even with that, I feel pretty lost.

I'm checking the numbers on the doors as I walk down a hallway, looking for freshman English, when I bump into a solid chest.

"Oh, sorry." I quickly step back and look up to apologize. I have to tilt my head back quite a ways before my eyes land on Clayton Dennison. I try to hide my grimace.

His eyes twinkle in amusement. "I was wondering if you were going to notice me here or just walk right into me. Guess it's my lucky day. I don't get pretty girls slamming into me every morning, you know."

My body tenses at his words. Is he seriously flirting with me? Doesn't he know better by now? Maybe he's just one of those guys who can't help it, like Brax Hilton.

"You were waiting for me to bump into you? You didn't think about stepping aside?"

Clayton shrugs, still smirking. "Are you lost? Where you headed?"

"Room 312." Clayton has an uncanny ability to show up just when I need rescuing. Not that I really need it right now, but I certainly don't want to be late for my first class, and, judging by the hurried steps of those still in the hallway, class is about to start.

Clayton nods. "That's Mack Hall." He points behind him and I spin to find open double doors.

"Thanks," I say shortly before hurrying inside. I don't look back at Clayton.

After I slip into a seat near the back, Caroline takes the one beside me. "Sweet, we're in the same class," I greet her with a grin.

"So, who was that guy in the hallway? You seemed to know him."

"Oh, yeah. He went to my high school. He's a senior."

"Damn, what's in the water at your high school, Pepper? It's a breeding ground for hot dudes. Your boyfriend, Ryan Harding, and that guy." She pretends to fan herself. Apparently Caroline is chatty when it's one on one. Interesting.

"Well, Ryan only moved to Brockton his senior year when his dad became the UC coach, but yeah, Brockton's got some hot guys, I won't argue with that." She should see Wesley Jamison, Jace's half-brother. He holds his own.

"It's like the home of the beautiful and athletic. A little different from my dumpy hometown."

"I thought you were from Las Vegas? Honestly, I didn't even know real people lived there."

She laughs. "A suburb of Vegas."

"Gotcha."

"So what sport does that guy in the hallway play? I know an athlete when I see one."

Sighing, I indulge her curiosity. "That's Clayton Dennison." I wait for a reaction and when I see she doesn't know who he is, I tell her. "He's the baseball pitcher. And he's probably going to the Major Leagues when he graduates."

She whistles under her breath. When the professor arrives and draws our attention to her, I'm relieved. Clayton Dennison is complicated. He's not someone I want to think about, and until today, I haven't really had to in a while.

Last year, Clayton had helped save me from crazy Savannah Hawkins. The first time, he got me out of a public situation when she drugged me – yes, she put roofies in my drink – during my official recruit visit at UC. The second time, he was the first at the scene when she hit me with her car. So when I say crazy, I mean *crazy*.

Before those episodes, Jace was worried Clayton was going to be a problem. In high school, Clayton's reign at Brockton Public was tainted by the presence of Jace Wilder, and when Jace became a student at UC last fall, the same thing was happening all over again for Clayton. Jace once again became the hottest athlete on campus as a freshman, and it looked like Clayton was going to target me in order to bring Jace down a notch.

But he must have changed his tune after realizing we had our own issues without his interference. Last time I asked Jace about Clayton, he said there was nothing going on there. Clayton backing off could also have been because Jace didn't really go out much, and kept a low profile. Clayton could still pretend to be the top dog in the social scene, though when Jace did show up at parties, it was an even bigger deal because it was so rare. Either way, Clayton backed off. At least, he had stopped his flirtations with me. Until today.

I would have to give Jace a heads-up. He didn't like it when I kept stuff like this from him, and after all we'd been through, I didn't blame him. Jace had stalkers and enemies and people who wanted to challenge him, felt threatened by him. Staying in the loop as to who these people were and what they had on their agenda was simply part and parcel of being with Jace Wilder. We'd had a reprieve from drama since the Savannah Hawkins showdown, but that didn't mean we were in the clear for good.

After my morning classes, I'm excited to meet Jace for lunch. He texted me this morning to meet him at Molly's Deli. It's off campus, which allows us to eat together without all our teammates. I like that he makes time for just the two of us, especially today, my first day of college classes. I'm already worried about all my assignments and I want to vent my worries to Jace and get his take on the syllabi for the classes I've had so far.

Jace isn't waiting for me when I arrive, so I find a little table in the back and wait. It feels good to take off my backpack. College text books are seriously heavy and we don't have lockers to go to between classes like high school. Ten minutes later, and still no Jace. I've checked my phone for a text, because he's rarely late to meet me, but there's nothing. Eventually, my stomach is growling so I order two sandwiches. Maybe by the time Jace gets here they'll be ready.

But he never shows. I call him, text him, eat my sandwich. I'm a little worried. He always has his phone on him. I can't imagine he forgot our lunch date *and* his phone. Something must be up.

My anxiety increases as the day goes on, and when there's still no word by practice, it's morphed into anger. I'd take out my emotions on the workout, but it's just an easy recovery run today. The anger mixes with worry when I don't see him at Chapman Hall with the rest of his teammates at dinner.

Frankie, Jace's roommate, catches my eye from across the cafeteria. He tilts his head toward the hallway leading to the restrooms and I nod. My heart is racing when I see his stern expression. I try not to let my mind wander but all I can think is that he's in the hospital. That something horrible happened to him. I don't know why my mind goes straight there, but it does.

I find Frankie's large frame leaning against the wall, arms crossed. We stand facing one another, each searching the other's expression.

"Jace missed practice today," Frankie tells me quietly. "Do you know where he is?"

"He missed a lunch date with me, too. And I haven't heard anything from him since this morning."

Frankie, who is usually playful and friendly, curses harshly under his breath. "He's never missed a practice. He's the quarterback. The practice today was supposed to be centered around him. The coaches were pissed. Beyond pissed."

A shiver runs down my spine. Even when Jace was partying hard in high school, he was still extremely committed to football. Something is very wrong. "Has anyone been able to get in touch with him?"

Frankie shakes his head. "We left our place together this morning. He had Business Management first thing, I know that."

"My roommate is in that class," I say. "I'll see if she saw him there. But honestly, she would have told me if there was anything weird."

Frankie hunches his shoulders, nodding. It's disconcerting seeing such a big guy freaked out like this. He's Jace's sidekick in college, and at times acts like his personal bodyguard. A small part of me is comforted that someone else is worried about Jace, but mostly I'm trying not to hyperventilate with panic.

I haven't touched my dinner yet, but after talking with Frankie the thought of food makes me nauseated. My stomach is in knots. I pull Lexi away from the group and ask if Jace was in class today.

"Yeah, I saw him. He said hi. Why?"

"Did you notice anything off?"

She thinks for a moment before responding. "Not that I can think of."

"Did you see where he went after class?"

She shakes her head. "It's a big class. What's going on?"

I rub my temples, feeling a headache coming on. "I'll tell you later, okay? I just, I need to get going for now."

Lexi blinks at me a few times, trying to figure me out, but I just grab my dinner tray and dump the food on my way out. Gina would be pissed if she saw how much food I wasted, but that's the least of my concerns right now.

As soon as I leave the cafeteria, I realize that my search and rescue plans will be difficult to execute without a car. I've gotten so used to not needing a car on campus, it's easy to forget that some places are a lot easier to get to with one. I spin around and head back inside. Trying to ignore the curious looks from Jace's teammates, I find Frankie sitting with the team. His back is to me and I have to tap him awkwardly on the shoulder to get his attention.

He turns to look at me, confused. I open my mouth to ask if we can use his car, but the silence at the table makes me hesitate. Everyone is watching us, wondering what I'll say. They know I'm Jace's girlfriend, and they know he wasn't at practice today. A lump forms in my throat. I don't want to fuel the rumor mill. Frankie finally realizes my dilemma and stands up, placing a hand on my shoulder and steering me away.

When we're out of earshot, I ask if he wouldn't mind driving me around to look for Jace, and he agrees at once. We're out the door, in his car, and driving down Shadow Lane within minutes. Jace and I grew up on Shadow Lane, a residential street not far from the UC campus. We pass my apartment building, where Gran still lives, and pull up to the Wilders' bi-level house. Jace's Jeep isn't here, but maybe his dad, Jim, will have some answers.

Frankie follows me to the door, and when no one answers, I punch in the garage code. Frankie doesn't question me when I lead him to Jace's old bedroom on the lower floor. He doesn't live here anymore, but it's still his. As I begin to rummage through his closet and drawers, Frankie asks roughly, "What are you looking for?"

Sighing, I throw up my hands. "I have no idea!"

Frankie smiles at me, amused by my frantic search for nothing in particular. I can't help my smile back. "This is stupid. I just thought I might find some clue about where he went."

"Is it weird his dad isn't home?"

"No, Jim has a new girlfriend and he's probably with her." Jim dated a woman named Sheila for over a year, but he's been back on the market for a few months. I can't tell if this new one is going to be serious or not. Jim's dating life has never really affected his relationship with his son or with me, so it doesn't matter much to me.

"Well, where to next, then?" Frankie asks.

"His mom's place."

"Lead the way."

No one's at Annie's apartment either, and I don't have a key to investigate, so we head to the library next. Jace sometimes studies at the Brockton Public Library, where his mom works, instead of at the campus libraries. But when we get there, we discover it's closed for the night.

We sit in the parking lot, quiet. "Any other ideas?" Frankie's voice is soft.

I shake my head before checking my phone for the zillionth time. Nothing. Lexi tried calling once, but that's it. We could go to my apartment – my old home – on Shadow Lane, but I don't want to alarm Gran. Not yet, at least.

"Maybe we should just go back to our places and wait for him to show up or call us, huh?" Frankie offers.

"Or we could keep driving around town to every spot he might be," I suggest. I'm only half-kidding. Though driving around is unlikely to be fruitful, the idea of waiting in my dorm room for him depresses me. I'm wound tight with worry by now.

"Should we check the hospital or the jail?" I wonder.

Frankie's whole body freezes at this. "You think?"

"I don't know what else to do." My voice is shaking and wobbly and I hardly recognize it.

"What about calling his parents?"

I've already thought of that. "I'm giving it another hour before I call them." At this point, I can't imagine anything other than an emergency is keeping Jace from answering his phone or telling anyone where he'd be. But something is stopping me from calling in the forces. Campus security, the police, his parents, Gran... it's just too much. "One more hour, and then we'll call in reinforcements, okay?"

"It's just, his parents might know where he is," Frankie offers.

"I know, we'll call them soon."

Frankie backs out of his parking spot, returning to campus. There's still a small part of me that hopes this is all some wild misunderstanding. That Jace had some first-day-of-school field trip he forgot about and didn't bring his phone. Or maybe his car broke down somewhere and his phone battery died. Nothing really makes sense though, because cell phones are easy to borrow from people, and he could have called someone – me, Frankie, his coach – to let us know what was going on. All I can think is that he's unconscious somewhere, unable to get help. That he was hit by a car and left on the side of the road. Images of his bloody body assault me as the possibilities run through my mind. Before I know it, we've pulled into my dorm parking lot and my entire body is shaking.

Frankie places his hand on my arm. "Pepper, you're white as a sheet, let me walk you up."

I shake my head. "No, you should go back to your place. Maybe Jace is there. Maybe he fell asleep by accident or something. Check his room."

Frankie watches me cautiously as I climb out of his car. My body won't stop shaking as I make my way up three flights of stairs. All I can think is that Jace is most likely in the hospital. Hurt. Broken.

I can't lose him. I just can't. He's my best friend. Family. And the love of my life. I can't even imagine a world without Jace Wilder in it.

A surge of panic and pain hits me as I reach the landing, and I have to clutch the wall not to stumble backward and fall down the stairs. But just as I start to lose my balance, firm, strong arms catch me around the waist and hold me in place.

The familiar scent of laundry detergent and pine body wash assaults me and the relief is so bone deep that I do actually lose my footing, collapsing.

"Jace," I whisper. "You're here."

CHAPTER SIX

"I'm here," he murmurs, and a new scent hits me. Liquor.

I turn to face him. His eyes dart over my face, confusion and something else showing in him.

"Have you been drinking?" I don't even try to fight the accusatory tone in my voice. What the hell? I thought he was dying or something. And he was drinking? My previous pain and desperation are quickly replaced by red-hot fury.

Jace blinks, as if in a trance. When a couple of girls race pass us in the stairwell, giggling, Jace lifts me up off my feet. "Let's go to your room to talk."

"I can walk fine." I resist his hold and break free, fishing my keys out of my pocket as we enter the common area of our suite. Lexi is sitting on the couch with Gina. Both look up from reading their textbooks when we come in. I smile tightly without saying a word, heading straight to my room.

Jace follows me and when we're alone in my room, I spin to face him. "First you need to call Frankie," I order harshly. "We were about to call the police." Okay, so we hadn't actually discussed calling the police, but he needs to realize how worried we were. Terrified, in fact.

"Can I use your phone?" he asks.

I hand it over to him, watching him closely as he scrolls through my contacts and finds Frankie. Though I'm eager for an explanation, if Frankie was half as worried as I was, he deserves to know Jace is here, in one piece.

I watch Jace carefully as he talks to Frankie. He apologizes, but he doesn't sound especially guilty, and offers no explanation. Frankie must not push him, because the phone call ends in less than a minute.

As soon as he's off, I cross my arms and let loose. "What the hell, Jace? Where have you been? First, you're a no-show at lunch with no explanation, then I find out from Frankie you ditched practice without telling a soul." I'm yelling and I'm sure my roommates can hear, but I couldn't care less. He's just standing there, hardly showing any emotion. He's put up a wall, I can see that immediately. He hasn't done this to me in a long time. And I'm determined to break through it.

"Frankie and I drove around town looking all over for you. I was about to start searching the hospital and the jail. I thought you were dead!" Okay, so I'm being a bit dramatic. I realize I'm even crying now. A complete and total hot mess. But does he have any idea how scared he had me? And he just shows up with liquor on his breath, completely unharmed?

Jace's wall is still there when he approaches me. He doesn't have far to go in my tiny dorm room. But when he says, "I'm sorry," it doesn't make me feel any better. I want his comfort more than anything, but he's still rigid, giving away nothing.

"Well? Are you going to tell me what's going on? Where you've been and why you didn't tell anyone?" I still sound hysterical. His closeness would normally calm me but with the way he's acting, he might as well be a brick wall.

"I went to the library after my morning class," he says calmly. "I didn't have another class for a while and I thought I'd stop by and bring some coffee to Annie before meeting you for lunch."

Immediately, I tense at that name. *Annie.* His mother. He's been calling her "Mom" for a long time now, but she's Annie again. This can't be good.

"She wasn't at the library. The other librarian said she didn't show up for work and wasn't answering her phone. So I went to Annie's apartment." He is so matter-of-fact, like he's relaying someone else's story. "It was locked but I have a key. When I went in, everything was gone. It was empty." His voice cracks slightly, and that tells me he's not entirely numb. But mostly, I'm shocked by what he's just said.

"Empty?" I repeat, unsure I'm understanding correctly.

"Empty. A few things in the fridge, and that's it."

"When was the last time you saw her?"

"Sunday morning. We had breakfast. She was a little distant, but I didn't think much of it."

"So what did you do when you saw her place was empty? Did you get in touch with her?"

He shakes his head. "While you were looking for me, I was looking for her. I'm sorry I didn't call. But, um, I broke my phone."

He's looking down at his feet sheepishly, but I still ask. "How did it break?"

"I threw it against the wall at Annie's place," he admits.

This doesn't surprise me, but it does send another round of pain through me on Jace's behalf, knowing how upset he must have been to find Annie's place empty. I don't mention that he could've found another means to reach me, Frankie, or his coach.

His excuse isn't good enough for me to instantly forgive him, but I can't even imagine what he's thinking and feeling right now. All I know is that I hurt so much for him. His mother just abandoned him. Again. After rebuilding his trust. The pain I feel for Jace cuts me deep, but I stand strong for him.

"Where did you look?" I ask quietly, gently, like my voice might send him over the edge. God, and I was yelling at him a moment ago.

His head snaps up and for the first time since he found me in the stairwell, emotion flashes across his face. Anger. Fury. It's utterly unfiltered rage, and it has me gasping in shock. And fear.

"I went to the fucker's office," he bites out. It takes me a second to realize he means Lance, whom we haven't spoken of since we met him over two weeks ago. "First thing I saw were the photos of his wife and kids on his desk, on the walls, all over the office. And his fucking wedding band." As quickly as the emotions flashed, he has detached himself again. I don't doubt that the anger is simmering just beneath the surface. I'm almost afraid to hear the rest of this story.

"I asked him where Annie was but he acted like he had no idea what I was talking about. I pressed hard, but I think he was telling the truth."

I skim Jace up and down now, but see no signs of physical violence. Still, I have to ask. "Did you hurt him?"

"I threw a few punches where it counts. He'll be hurting for a few weeks but I'm holding off with the threat to tell his family about his affair. I need to keep that to hold over him."

"Jace! You could get in serious trouble for assault. You could lose your scholarship." You could lose everything, I want to tell him. All because of his mother.

He doesn't react. "That's what I mean. He won't press charges because then I would tell his wife about the affair. Or she'll figure it out from the charges on her own."

This is messed up. Jace was calculated. He went to some virtual stranger's office and beat the crap out of him. He expects no repercussions. Or he simply doesn't care. It's the possibility of the latter that really has me worried. If he destroyed his phone and threw punches, that means he really lost it.

"He told me Annie found out he was married two days ago, on Monday." She left because of that? She abandoned her only son, for a second time, because she had an affair with a married man? I knew she was a weak and selfish person. I *knew* it.

"I've been trying to find out where the fuck she went all day. All I can think is she relapsed, was ashamed to admit it, and is hiding out. I have to find her before it's too late."

"Too late for what?" She's gone, Jace. It's already too late.

"A relapse is okay, she can still get back on track. But she needs help or else she'll fall back into that lifestyle. If I find her, she might still have her apartment, her job." Jace might still be able to forgive her, keep the relationship they've been building for over a year now.

"Maybe she'll come back." But I don't really mean it. She's gone. I am certain of it.

"If I don't hear from her tomorrow, I'm filing a missing person's report," Jace announces.

"I was about to do the same for you," I blurt, still angry. Maybe it's mostly directed at his mother, but I hate that she can make him completely forget everything else in his world. That she has that power over him. I know that he's trying to forget the world around him because he's protecting himself. Because if he takes his focus off finding her, he will feel so much hurt it might break him. He's in denial that she's really gone, and I'm not sure how to deal with that. Do I help him stay in denial? I'm really scared what will happen when he comes out of it.

Jace doesn't stay. He doesn't want my comfort. I'm not even sure why he came in the first place. He simply leaves, saying he needs to get back to his apartment and call his coach. I know I shouldn't be hurt by his coldness, that this is how he's coping, but I wish he would let me be there for him, like he always is for me. It feels like rejection in the worst way. Like I'm not enough.

Logically, I know that there is nothing like a mother's love. Gran explained this to me once. Even though my own mother is dead, I still had her love, and in a way, I still do. She never gave me up voluntarily. I try to crack open a book, knowing that getting behind on my school work the very first day of college classes is a bad idea, but I can't focus.

Instead, I poke my head into the common area of our four-bedroom dorm suite to see if anyone's around. Lexi and Gina have put their books aside and are watching TV. I join them on the couch, a bowl of popcorn between them.

"Want some?" Lexi offers me the bowl and I gladly take a handful. I try to pass it back, but neither girl wants any and I end up eating the rest of it myself. They're watching a reality show. Not my thing, but better than homework. It's not doing much to distract me from the anger burning inside me. I just can't believe Annie would disappear like this without telling Jace. It's messed up.

"The yellow house is having people over tonight, if you guys want to go do something," Gina suggests. Though I'm beat from the first day of classes and the emotional drain of searching for Jace, hanging out with the cross country guys sounds like a great way to get out of this funk.

Caroline opts to get started on her homework, but Gina and Lexi aren't in the mood to study either. I don't know if it's because they're sophomores, and more confident that they can get their schoolwork done eventually, or if they are just the type of people who rarely do homework. Either way, I'm happy to be going somewhere that will get me out of my own head.

Gina is the only one of us with a car, and while we could easily walk to the yellow house, we opt for laziness. I like that none of us bother changing out of our casual clothes or putting on makeup. I know this isn't a party or anything, but it's still a bunch of guys, and most girls would take a few minutes to stare at themselves in the mirror first.

When we get to the house, we find that we aren't the only ones still in denial that classes have started. The house isn't packed, but it's more than just the cross team here. Lexi heads straight for the fridge and helps herself to a beer. "Want one?" she asks.

Without thinking, I say sure. It's been a long day, and it's not like I'll be making this a habit. Besides, everyone else in the house seems to have a drink. Gina goes for water though, and I notice Lexi scrutinizing her. Before I can determine what Lexi is thinking, a loud group of girls passes through the kitchen.

My body tenses when I recognize two of them. One is tall and slim, with unmistakable frizzy black hair. Her soft blue eyes land on me before quickly darting away. Her name is Lizzie Valentine and she was with Frankie the night we discovered Savannah in Jace's dorm room. She was a key witness in the police report, and was one of the reasons her former teammate got expelled from UC and pleaded guilty to several crimes against me. I'm not sure what happened to her after that. I never saw her again with Frankie, and he never mentioned her.

But it's a different girl who makes me clench the bottle of beer in my hand and stand up straighter, preparing myself for a confrontation. The last few times I saw her, she was wearing pigtail braids. Now, she sports a single dark brown braid down her back. Her name is Veronica Finch, and Savannah was her best friend.

Despite everything Savannah did to me, Veronica still blames *me* for Savannah's expulsion and jail time. She made this clear when I ran into her at a coffee shop last spring. When she turns our way, she sneers at me, but doesn't slow her pace on the way to the living room.

"Do you know them?" Gina asks me.

I shake my head. "Not exactly."

"Oh come on," Lexi calls me out. "Veronica Finch hates you because her crazy-ass friend stalked you and your boyfriend. She and Savannah were on a psycho world-domination mission. Or Brockton domination. Most know Veronica's cray-cray, but some of her teammates probably still side with her because they were bummed to lose Savannah. For all her psycho, she was a sick soccer player."

Gina watches my reaction, and I sigh, defeated. Gina puts an uncharacteristically gentle arm on my shoulder. "Don't worry about it, you've got your own team to stick up for you now."

And with that reassurance, we head into the living room area. I'm relieved it's mostly familiar cross teammates hanging out. Lexi points out a half-dozen guys who are on the soccer team, but aside from them and some soccer girls, there are no new faces.

Veronica knows I'm here, but she must think better of confronting me when we're essentially on my territory. Instead, she's spotted Brax Hilton and she begins making her way over to him. Brax doesn't notice her because he's grinning at Lexi heading in his direction.

"Hey ladies!" he greets us with such enthusiasm that the rest of the room turns to look our way. "Nicely done, getting one of your freshman roommates to come out on her first night of classes." Brax fist-bumps Lexi and Gina and then envelops me in a hug. I see Lexi frowning from over his shoulder, and I imagine she's put off by the fist bump. That's not really something you do with the girl you're hooking up with.

When he releases me, Veronica is at his side. Though I'm tempted to stand my ground, I really don't feel like dealing with her tonight. As Veronica steals Brax's attention, Lexi ditches him in favor of a couple of the guys on the soccer team. I gladly follow her, but refrain from participating in the blatant flirting going on.

This get-together isn't so different from the few other college parties I've been to in the past with Jace. It seems to me that everyone is here to flirt and find someone to hook up with. I guess I was hoping for some low-key hanging out with my teammates. We haven't had much comradery outside of practice and meals yet. But everyone here seems to have a purpose, except for me. Well, I do have a purpose, but it's not the same as Lexi's, Brax's, Veronica's, and the guys' we are currently standing beside, who seem to know I'm taken, and are rivaling for Lexi's attention.

I actually feel a little left out, but it's not like I genuinely want to be looking for a casual hookup. I just don't feel like I'm really supposed to be here. I should be with Jace. He's had what might just be the worst day of his life. And it wasn't the best day for me, either. Yet Jace doesn't want to be with me right now.

I should be his rock. I should be comforting him, loving him. Instead, he disappeared all day and as soon as I found him, he was gone just as quickly. My stomach flips uneasily in concern, but I can't control how Jace copes with what's happened. I can't force him to come to me.

CHAPTER SEVEN

My beer goes down easily and I head to the kitchen to get a second one. Though the soccer guys offer to get us another round, I won't take drinks from strangers after what happened to me at Alberto's last year. I decide that instead of sulking, I can find great entertainment simply observing the interactions at the yellow house.

As I return to the living room, I glance to Veronica and Brax and find myself stifling a giggle. It appears Veronica is petting Brax's arm, but he's mostly ignoring her, his gaze drifting to Lexi. If she's trying to get his attention by talking to other guys, it's working. Brax's heated expression does not reflect someone who is only interested in a casual hookup, and I can't help but wonder if Lexi realizes this. It only takes a moment after I rejoin Lexi for Brax to appear between us.

He doesn't touch her, but his stance signals that he won't be leaving her side any time soon. He's not in a position to get all territorial, but simply by standing there, slightly leaning over her, he's showing Lexi and these two guys that he will be very displeased if the flirting continues.

The next few minutes are excruciatingly awkward. I think we're all equally relieved when Lexi drags me off to the bathroom with her. But when she's got us locked in there and plops herself on the edge of the tub, it's not Brax she wants to talk about.

"Dude, what do you think about Gina?"

"Gina?" I repeat, confused. Why is she asking about our roommate? I'm immediately uncomfortable. So far, I really like Lexi and I see us becoming close friends. But if she's the kind of girl who drags me off to bathrooms to bad-mouth our roommate, I'm going to have to start questioning whether she's best friend material.

Lexi bites her nails, something I've noticed she does when nervous or stressed. "Yeah, Gina Waters, our roommate? What's your impression of her these past couple of weeks?"

Lexi's nervousness makes me think this is more than idle gossip or bad-mouthing, and I decide to answer honestly. Her probing question gives me reason to hesitate, but she's otherwise given me every reason to trust her.

"Gina's hard to read," I admit. "She can be sort of grumpy and snappy but once in a while she'll be real sweet. Maybe she's just a little uptight? Takes herself a bit too seriously? I don't know. I mean, I like her, I just get the feeling she doesn't really want to be my friend or something."

I do like Gina. Despite making somewhat snide remarks from time to time, she doesn't seem to have any agenda. That's hard to find.

"You haven't noticed anything else? Anything weird?"

"Besides what I just told you? What are you getting at, Lexi?" My patience is wearing down.

"Look, I probably shouldn't say anything, but I just can't keep it to myself."

"I don't like the sound of this," I admit. The last thing I want is to be drawn into drama between Gina and Lexi. They are my teammates and roommates, and they were friends with each other before I came along.

"I need another opinion," Lexi says, and there's pleading in her voice. "I'm worried about Gina, okay? She's been acting a lot different since we got back from summer break. She was never snappy before, like you said she is. I wanted an impression from someone who didn't know her last year. She may not have ever been in the running for a friendliest-girl-in-the-world award but she definitely wasn't as stand-offish last year."

I wait, wondering where this is going. "So, you're worried about her bad attitude?"

"I think she has an eating disorder," Lexi finally blurts out.

It clicks. Once those words are said, it's serious. A lot of runners are thin and have very minimal body fat. I'm considered underweight by official weight and height charts, and I'm sure most girls on our team are as well. Gina is also thin, but not startlingly so. Lexi must have her reasons, though. Because any of our teammates, including me and Lexi, could be told we need to gain weight. Well, Gran has been telling me that my entire life. But none of us want to be told we have an eating disorder.

"It's not just how she's acting, okay? She's definitely watching what she eats way more than she was before. I mean, the girl hasn't had a drink yet since we got back to campus. We used to eat popcorn together every night, and she never tells me she doesn't want any, so I make a bowl but she doesn't eat any of it."

"I can relate to not drinking," I tell Lexi. Accusing someone of an eating disorder because they don't drink beer or eat popcorn seems a bit overdramatic, but I don't say that. "It's okay to be a little stricter about eating snacks and stuff," I offer. I'm not sure why I'm inclined to play devil's advocate here, but Lexi seems to have drawn a fairly drastic conclusion. When Lexi continues biting her nails, I ask, "Has she lost weight?"

"A little, not a ton." When someone knocks on the door, Lexi sighs. "Maybe I'm overreacting."

"Just a minute," I tell whoever is at the door. "It's okay to be worried," I reassure her. "But it could be something different that's making her moody, or nothing at all."

Lexi shrugs. "Yeah, I just have a bad feeling. She's not herself."

There's more banging. "Hurry up, you guys!" It's Zeb. "Some of us are heading out to Alberto's and I gotta grab something from in there."

Lexi and I glance at each other. "What exactly do you need to grab, Zeb?" Lexi asks as she opens the door.

"Condoms," he says simply. He opens a closet inside the bathroom, full of towels, shampoo bottles, and a very large box of condoms. Lexi raises her eyebrows at me as Zeb pulls out several and stuffs them in his pocket. When he turns around and finds us watching him, he shrugs. "What?"

"Nothing," we say in unison.

He rolls his eyes and heads back to the living room. Everyone is finishing their drinks and talking about walking to Alberto's, a popular campus bar. People have congregated there in an impromptu party. I'm not ready to head home when the house begins to clear out, but I don't have a fake ID to get me into the bar. And even if I did, I have no interest in returning to the place where Savannah drugged my drink last fall.

Gina offers me her keys to drive home, but I've had two beers, and I'd rather walk. I'm not thrilled about walking home by myself, but I'm prepared to do so when Ryan comes downstairs with Kiki, our team captain, behind him. They aren't holding hands or touching, but the few of us remaining in the living room can tell what they've been up to. The two of them have been noticeably absent since we arrived.

So when Ryan offers to drive me home, and Kiki joins Brax, Gina and Lexi to head out to Alberto's, I'm more than a little confused. They just hooked up, probably even had sex, yet they didn't even say goodbye to each other. Is this how it works in college? Boom, bang, done? Do Kiki and Ryan hook up a lot and just act like it never happens at practice? Sex has always been very personal between me and Jace. We've known each other our entire lives, and dated for nearly a year before I gave him my virginity. Maybe I'm not like other girls, or maybe things are different in college.

Either way, I find myself alone with Ryan in his Jeep, the same one we used to make out in years ago when we dated, only minutes after he likely slept with my team captain. It's a lot to take in.

We're quiet during the drive. He's changed, I know that now. He's more serious, more contemplative, than he was in high school. He doesn't say anything to lighten the awkwardness, like he might have before. And the Sufjan Stevens song playing from the speakers only serves to make the atmosphere more somber.

As Ryan pulls up in front of my building, I suddenly want to be anywhere but in my dorm room. It sounds so lonely and depressing. Most of my friends are at Alberto's and my boyfriend would rather be alone than with me right now. When Ryan simply says, "See you tomorrow," I know I've been dismissed.

"Thanks for the ride," I tell him before shutting the door. He's shown no interest in friendship, and I can't blame him. I essentially told him that we need to keep our distance since I have a boyfriend and he's my ex. I meant that we needed to stay at arm's length, but he understood it to mean we should stop communicating. So, it was nice of him to give me a ride, but I shouldn't expect more.

As soon as he's pulled away, though, I find myself walking right past the door to my building and in the direction of Jace's apartment. It's not exactly around the corner, but I'm still worried about him. I won't be able to sleep tonight in my current mindset. I shoot him an email to let him know I'm stopping by, since he's got no phone for the moment, but by the time I show up at his apartment twenty minutes later, he hasn't responded.

When I knock, no one answers. There's no light or sound coming through, and, seeing it's nearly midnight, I'm hoping that means he's asleep.

An unexpected wave of loneliness accompanies me on my walk back from Jace's apartment. It's a beautiful September night. Not exactly warm, but not chilly yet either. I cut through the main quad and it's the first time I've seen it completely empty. There are no sounds but my breathing and my steps on the sidewalk. No other people around. I don't want to be alone right now. The ache in my chest grows and I recognize it for what it is.

Homesickness.

I'm in my hometown, only a few miles from the apartment where I grew up, yet I know that the pit in my stomach is a craving for familiarity.

My new friends and teammates are great but that's the thing – they are new. They don't know me inside and out like my old friends. Like Gran. Like Jace. It's why I want to cuddle in bed with him right now. He's comfort. Strength. Love. Annie leaving him hurts me deeply.

Because she left me, too. And if I feel this hurt and angry, I can't even imagine how Jace is feeling.

I wish I could call Jace to check in, but he's trashed his phone and I don't want to bother Frankie. Something doesn't feel right, and it haunts me through the night. It's a fitful sleep, and I'm beyond groggy when I stumble to the bathroom in the morning. Lexi joins me a moment later, still in her outfit from the night before.

"Good night?" I ask, my voice muffled as I brush my teeth.

"Yeah, just got back."

"Brax?" I ask.

"Yeah, it's becoming, like, a thing, now, I guess," she says. I don't know what that means, but I'm not sure she does either. "Practice is gonna be a bitch today," she tells me as she goes into a stall. "Half the team was at Alberto's until closing and I for one had too much to drink."

"We aren't supposed to have a workout today though, right?" I double-check.

"Ugh, we might," she says as she pees. "Sometimes Coach pulls a fast one on us and decides it's an excellent day to do hill repeats."

I groan. I've been holding my own so far but with my lack of sleep, hill sprints would kick my butt.

Lexi finishes her business and washes her hands before grabbing her toothbrush. "Alberto's was packed last night. That always happens when your boyfriend shows up."

My stomach drops. "Jace was there?"

Lexi glances at me in the mirror. I try to sound casual, but she can probably hear the surprise in my voice. "Yeah. Everyone was there, dude. We had to wait forever to get in the door. But they had the back patio open so a lot more people can fit. I think Gina busted out of there pretty quick though. She gets jumpy when it's that crowded."

"Yeah." It's all I can muster. Jace was out partying while I was here worried and hurting for him? I want to be pissed, but I can't be. Because I know exactly how he felt. I wanted to be out with lots of people too last night. Often, I want to be alone when I'm hurting or emotionally overwhelmed. Actually, I usually cope by running, but I'm working on curbing that impulse, as it's not always the healthiest outlet given how much I already run with the team. But last night, I didn't want to be alone. Not at all. I wanted Jace. And he wanted to be with everyone else. It hurts, but I can't be angry. How can I judge someone who was just abandoned by his mom for a second time?

JACE

Frankie's on his way out of our apartment when I get there. He watches me closely, trying to read my mood. If he thinks he can figure me out, he's going to be disappointed.

"Stop looking at me like that, man," I tell him with a lightness in my voice that softens the demand. "I'm sorry I fucked with your head today, and I'll apologize to the team. It was family stuff. And no, I don't fucking want to talk about it. Where are you headed?"

Frankie shakes his head, looking almost like my father does when he's resigned to me being a punk-ass kid. I don't appreciate it.

"Are you going to ground me or something?" I'm hoping to smooth over everything without actually addressing what went down today.

"You want me to brush this off?" Frankie doesn't hide the hurt in his voice. He's a little like Pepper that way. Tough but sensitive. "Why aren't you with your girl right now?"

I step back, unprepared for that question, or its answer. I don't know the answer and I'm certainly not going soul-searching to find it. "Is that your business?" This time my tone is not playful.

Frankie doesn't back down. "She was shaking, man. She was really scared for you. Go make it right," he tells me.

"I'm going to Alberto's," I announce, walking away from him. "You can come if you want."

He follows me, but we don't speak for a few blocks. "Look, dude," I finally break the silence. "You were crazy about that girl on the soccer team last year. What was her name?"

"Lizzie," he murmurs.

I know her name, but I want to make sure he's with me. "Do I ask you what happened with her? Do I tell you to stop being scared and using what happened with Savannah as an excuse not to go after her? No. That's your business, Frankie."

Lizzie and Frankie were on the precipice of something serious when they walked in on Savannah Hawkins attempting to seduce me in my dorm room last fall. Frankie prevented Savannah from attacking Pepper that night, and Lizzie's testimony ensured Savannah's guilt in the criminal case. But as far as I know, Frankie stopped hooking up with Lizzie after it all went down. It wasn't out of loyalty to me, because I made a point of telling him I was totally cool with him being with my stalker's former soccer teammate. I'm not the most perceptive dude when it comes to people's relationships and it was obvious even to me that Frankie wanted Lizzie bad, and he was afraid of rejection. But I didn't call him out on it.

Frankie throws a beefy arm over my shoulder. "I get what you're saying, Wilder," he says gruffly before pulling away. "But next time maybe you *should* just tell me to grow some balls, okay?"

I laugh. "Yeah, maybe I will. But that doesn't mean you've got permission to tell *me* what to do."

A couple hours later and I've had more shots in one night than I've had the entire year. Frankie's drinking harder than usual too, but when Lizzie walks in, he switches to water, and I can practically feel the dude working up his courage next to me.

"Frankie, you don't have to stay at my side all damn night. Grow a pair," I finally tell him.

He's over there talking to her a moment later, and the girl is clearly excited about it. I take some satisfaction that at least someone's night is going well. When Veronica Finch approaches me, I'm almost happy for the target. Veronica was best friends with Savannah, and my instincts say she didn't entirely disapprove of what Savannah did.

She feigns shyness, but I'm not fooled. "Hi Jace," she says quietly.

I don't respond and she twirls a stray hair around her finger, pretending like she doesn't know what to say next. The girl has probably practiced the speech she's about to deliver in front of the mirror a million times. It begins with, "I'm so sorry about Savannah. You know I had no idea what she was up to..." and goes on and on. It's been nine months since her friend pleaded guilty to a handful of charges against me and Pepper, and apparently Veronica's been lying low waiting for things to cool off before firing up for another round.

When she finishes her speech, I remain calm. I'm indifferent to her apologies, but I'm far from detached about the words I deliver. "I haven't gone after you yet, Veronica, because you haven't been a problem. Savannah's gone, and whether you knew what she was doing can remain irrelevant. But only if you stay away from me."

Veronica nods, and I can see she senses the severity of what I'm saying.

"If you do anything to Pepper, I will hear about it, and I will ruin you. If she is hurt and I have any reason at all to suspect you're responsible, your soccer career and your life at UC will be over. So stay from me and stay away from Pepper. That's all I'm saying."

I don't think I'm being at all unreasonable here. Her best friend could have killed my girlfriend. And if Veronica Finch was the slightest bit sympathetic to Savannah Hawkins's scheme, she's dangerous. I've had some eyes and ears on her, but I'm definitely ramping that up now that Pepper's here on campus. I'm not taking any chances with her safety. Last year's shit was out of my control, and I almost lost her because of it. That will not happen again.

CHAPTER EIGHT

Lexi called it. Coach says they're hill sprints but this isn't a hill. The vertical incline is far too steep to be labeled something as benign as a hill. Cliff would be more accurate. Or at least, that's what it feels like. I'm too delirious to tell who is hungover, and besides, all of us are suffering. And we're only halfway through.

Aside from when I got injured last year, it's the first time I've ever seriously considered dropping out of a workout. My body rebels against me as Coach blows the whistle for the sixth of ten sprints. My temples throb from a massive headache. It's not a hangover, just fatigue and stress. Or maybe it *is* a hangover, I wouldn't know, but it seems unlikely from two beers.

The incline begins about two miles into the woods, and the trail is not well-maintained. We have to hop over several logs and rocks along the way. It's only wide enough to go up single file, but none of us are in a hurry to pass each other. I'm pumping my arms hard, keeping my head down to avoid tripping, when I slam into Trish, who has stopped abruptly in front of me. We manage to stay on our feet, and Lexi narrowly misses crashing into me and sending all three of us to the ground. As I move forward again, I hear the distinct sound of Trish throwing up.

My best guess is that it's from having one too many at Alberto's, though this workout could drive anyone to puking, hungover or not.

But Trish is back at it a moment later, patting me on the back and claiming she feels a heck of a lot better now. Each time we pass the bush she puked in on our way up, I feel my own wave of nausea hit.

I'm barely even running on the last sprint, if it can even be called that. Gran could probably walk faster as I struggle to reach the cones marking the end of the incline. None of us speak or look at each other as we jog back through the woods for our warm-down. Coach wasn't particularly encouraging either. He wasn't impressed with our performance.

I wish I could have been the one to pull the team through this excruciating workout. Something inside of me is burning to prove that I am a valuable member of this team. I've never had to do that before. Everyone around me is fast, tough, and capable of an amazing running career. I have high school accolades, but they don't matter here, in these woods, with these girls. I suffered just as much as the rest of my team through that workout, and I feel defeated.

When I show up at my apartment for dinner that night, Gran is surprised but overjoyed to see me. I need a break from my teammates, my concern for Jace, my uncertainty of what I mean to my new team.

I'm greeted by the familiar smell of a casserole cooking in the oven, and the feel of a wet nose at my knee when my dog, Dave, greets me. Gran's best friend Lulu is sitting at Jace's seat at the dinner table. Well, I think of it as Jace's seat, because he's sat there more than anyone else.

"You look exhausted, Salty," Lulu exclaims. It's her special nickname for me. A little weird, but hey, my actual name is pretty out there too.

"Bunny, get this girl a plate of that macaroni casserole. They aren't feeding her at the college."

Lulu is Gran's age – well into her seventies – and her hair is a different color every time I see her. Today, it's blue. With matching eyeshadow.

Gran plops an enormous heap of food in front of me before bombarding me with questions about classes, friends, running, and of course, Jace. I evade her questions about Jace, and I'm relieved when

Lulu begins asking about the attractiveness of college boys in general.

"I sure do miss the variety. We start to outlive 'em around now, and the selection pool gets smaller, you see."

Gran nods in agreement. "But Lulu and me, we don't let that stop our fun. Boy, you can find some real hunks at the senior center these days."

"It's that new retirement home they built, Bunny, I've told you this. It's attracting all the ranchers from the plains. And those ranchers, they've really kept their bodies in shape. Did you meet Wallace at the bowling alley the other night?"

"You mean the one in the cowboy hat and sweater vest? Why, he was buying me drinks all night! He's taking me to the steak house on Saturday," Gran announces proudly. "I think he's got some money, that one. He might be too refined for me, even for a cowboy."

It's a typical conversation between Lulu and Gran, meaning it doesn't make much sense. For one, I didn't know wealthy cowboys existed. For another, it seems unlikely a rancher would be named Wallace and also wear a cowboy hat with a sweater vest. But hey, what do I know?

Dinner with Gran and Lulu leaves me feeling warm and satisfied, and not just because her cooking is far superior to the food at Chapman Hall. Gran and Lulu are rolling a joint when I kiss them goodbye, and while I'm sure the rest of the night would be entertaining, I can't hide from reality forever.

Jace hasn't replaced his phone yet and I haven't had a chance to get a sense for where his head is at. So I decide to stop by his apartment. I'm not a huge fan of riding my bike at night after being the victim of a hit and run last year, but a car isn't in the budget and the town's simply too big to walk or run everywhere.

I find Jace sitting on the couch hunched over the coffee table, which is covered with papers. This would have been a rare sight in high school, but he's made a point of staying on top of his homework since becoming a college student. He glances up when he hears me open the door, and the soft smile that takes over his face sends a strong rush of relief through me. His expression is radiant and I'm so happy he hasn't shut down this piece of him. This sweet and loving side he reserves for me. I was worried it'd be a long time before I was able to bring it back.

"Hey, you," I greet him, returning the smile. I start to sit on the couch beside him but he pulls me into his lap.

"You look beat," he remarks, nuzzling that favorite spot underneath my ear.

"Yeah, Coach kicked our butts today at practice."

"I miss your butt," he rumbles, letting me know exactly what's on his mind.

Playful Jace carries me into his room and tosses me on his bed before shutting the door behind him. He's attentive and loving with every touch, and though he doesn't say the words, each caress feels like an apology. He doesn't let himself go until he's watched me look into his eyes. The wall he threw up yesterday is gone, and he's showing me just how deeply his emotions run. But they aren't about him or Annie. They are about us. Me. It's regret and tenderness in his eyes and the ferocity of it rips through me. For a brief moment I wonder if he's trying to tell me I matter more than his mother. *We* matter more. Because I've always been here for him. And she hasn't.

Jace keeps his body covering mine afterward and brushes his lips along my cheeks and forehead. He doesn't have to say anything. He handled things badly yesterday. And he doesn't need me to tell him I forgive him. Wrong or right, I can't help but forgive him.

"Are you hungry?" he asks.

"Actually, I'm craving brownies. Gran and Lulu were talking about baking some when I left."

"You were at Shadow Lane?" Jace refers to my home with Gran as the street that we both grew up on. I like that he does that. It means that our home is the same place, in a way.

"Yeah, I had dinner there."

Jace nods. "I didn't make it to Chapman. Stayed late working out to make up for yesterday."

"You haven't eaten?"

"Course I have. There's no way I was doing my homework hungry." Jace grins and raises a dark eyebrow. "You, on the other hand, I will do hungry, tired, sick…"

I shove him and he rolls over, pretending to fall off the bed before pulling on a pair of sweatpants. "Brownies, huh? Let's hit up the Union. It's open late and they've got burgers *and* brownies."

"Burgers? I thought you said you ate dinner already?" I search around the floor for my clothes and Jace finds them first, taking pleasure in helping me get dressed.

"That was my first dinner. Come on, Pep, you didn't meet me yesterday. I'm a two-dinner guy."

He finishes dressing me and I tease him about being like a hobbit with his multiple daily meals as we make our way out the door. This time when I cross the quad, my fingers intertwined with Jace's, I'm at peace. The loneliness and homesickness that assaulted me on this walk last night has disappeared as quickly as it arrived. The reality is that Jace is a piece of my home, and when things aren't right with him, it doesn't matter whether I'm in my hometown, I'll still feel off. Even in the warmth of Gran's kitchen, my heart and mind remain unsettled without him. This truth doesn't frighten me like it once might have. It just is. And perhaps I'm okay with it because I know it's the same truth for Jace too.

When we get to the Union, it's packed with students. I've only passed through here a couple of times, and I've never seen it so crowded. We order food at the counter and as we search for a spot to sit, my eyes land on Gina, who is alone at a high table in a far corner. The small round top is piled with food, and Gina's eyes are glued to an open book in her lap as she shoves French fries in her mouth. If Lexi was afraid Gina's dieting was too extreme, she doesn't need to worry. Of course, binge eating is a well-known element of some eating disorders too, but Lexi didn't express any concern with that. Gina is intent on reading her book, and her mindless munching makes me think she isn't as preoccupied with her diet as Lexi believes.

I'm hit with an unexpected wave of hunger when Jace grabs his burger from the counter and I catch a whiff of the wonderful smell of onion rings. It occurs to me that Gina probably just eats more meals at the Union instead of Chapman Hall because the food is better here.

Gina isn't sending out sociable vibes, and there aren't any open tables. But it doesn't take long before someone calls Jace's name, and a couple of empty chairs are pulled up to a busy table. I recognize most of the guys as Jace's teammates and I'm not surprised to find each of them with a plate of food. Several girls are at the table as well, but they aren't eating and I get the distinct impression they are football player groupies. It's the way they watch the guys at the table so eagerly, not to mention their provocative outfits, which are designed to send a certain message.

The captain, Dimitri Johnson, grins at us as we take our seats. "Wilder, you're going to have to start bringing Pepper here around more now that she's a college girl."

"Yeah man, are we going to see more of you outside practice now?" another asks before turning to me. "What do you think? Are you going to get this guy to party with us more?"

I shrug, a little uncomfortable. "I'm not his boss, just his girlfriend."

The guys think this is hilarious and Jace shakes his head before biting into his burger.

"She sure didn't have much control over him last night," a platinum blonde sitting beside Dimitri speaks up, and the laughter dies down. "Unless you guys have some kind of open relationship." The lightness in her tone is in direct contrast with the vicious words coming out of her mouth.

For a brief second, I'm inclined to reply with a snide comment and then forget her words. I've learned that girls can be mean and jealous when it comes to Jace Wilder, and that I can't take what they say seriously. But I know what happened to him yesterday. I saw how he shut down emotionally. A disturbing coldness washes through me and I vaguely recognize it as panic. Is there any truth to what she's implying? Was the apology in his touch earlier meant for more than being MIA yesterday?

"All right, Dani, if you're going to be a stuck-up bitch, get out of here." Dimitri's voice slices through the silence and I watch him practically shove her out of her chair. I'm startled by his harshness, though the way she tosses her hair behind her and smirks in my direction tells me she isn't sorry.

The awkwardness in her wake is palpable. No one knows what to say. Jace is a leader on his team and if he tries to defend himself from that comment in front of his teammates, he'll look weak. I'm certainly not about to confront him with an audience watching.

I don't know where to look and I'm staring at my brownie when a hand squeezes my shoulder. "Yo, Pepper, you and Harding made the smart choice turning it in early last night, huh?" Brax Hilton asks, oblivious to the tension at the table.

I swing my head toward him, grateful for the distraction. That is, until I sense Jace's body going rigid beside me, and the implication of Brax's question hits me.

"Yeah, I'm glad he gave me a ride home," I say, attempting to clarify any misunderstanding that could be taken from the question. "You guys who went out to Alberto's last night were suffering today at the hill sprints, huh?"

I don't mention that I didn't get any sleep either, and was probably just as poorly off.

"Dude, Coach always seems to pull that shit after the worst nights. He must take one look at us and know we're hungover."

I latch onto this welcome subject change. "I think Zeb still smelled like tequila."

Brax laughs. "Man, you're right." He takes in the rest of the people at the table then, but he's not intimidated. "No way Coach is doing that to us two days in a row though, so if you want to party tonight, go for it."

"Thanks for that, Brax, but I'm good."

He shrugs and waves before heading off, and it's only a moment before Jace finishes inhaling his meal and is hurrying us out of the Union.

As soon as we're back on the quad, alone on the sidewalk, he turns to face me. "We are *not* in an open relationship." Jace's voice is pleading and holds a note of authority I don't imagine most boyfriends would be able to pull off if in his shoes. After all, he was essentially just accused of cheating on me, on the same night where I spent all day unable to find him before he disappeared on me again. He shouldn't have the upper hand here, but somehow, his confidence comforts me.

"Then why should anyone think we are?" I ask in response.

Jace leans toward me. "They shouldn't. I was drunk. For just one night. *One* night," he emphasizes. "It's the first time I've ever been drunk in college, and girls thought it meant I wanted more. I didn't."

My eyes narrow and I cross my arms. I don't like this. Just the idea of girls being all over him makes me feel physically ill.

"I don't and I won't. We will *never* be an open relationship, Pepper," he says sternly.

His reassurances are enough for me. I trust him. But that doesn't mean I'm okay with this kind of situation repeating itself. "I'm not going to tell you not to drink or not to go out and party like your teammates do. But you're different from them. You're stronger but you're also more vulnerable. Because everyone is watching you, and wants to be a part of your life."

Jace is watching me speak, standing close, but not touching me. He knows what I mean. It's always been this way.

"You have to be careful." I'm about to talk to him about his mom, to tell him that no matter how much it hurts, he can't do anything to destroy what he's built – his position on the team, his relationship with me, the respect the people on this campus have for him. But despite how different he's been today, I don't think he's ready to talk about her yet.

"I *will* be careful," Jace promises, wrapping his hands around my waist and pulling me into his chest. "For you, I will be."

"For *us*," I clarify. "And for yourself."

CHAPTER NINE

Over the next few days, we each have an individual meeting with Coach Harding. Mine is one of the last, on Friday following a tempo workout that gave us all a chance to redeem ourselves after the torturous hill sprints.

The women's assistant coach, Susan, is also in the office when I knock lightly on the glass door. I've already showered and changed in the locker room while I waited for the other freshmen to have their meetings. No one really talks about their meetings, and I find myself incredibly nervous when I finally sit in the chair across from his desk.

Susan sits in a chair beside me, legs crossed, notebook in her lap, and she smiles reassuringly. Now in her forties, she's a former collegiate runner who was probably in my shoes at one point.

"How are things going so far, Pepper?" Coach Harding asks.

There are a lot of ways to interpret the question. "Good, I think? I mean, the girls on the team are great."

Coach nods. "It's a fine group of women. How do you feel you've been handling the workouts?"

I sit up straighter in my chair. Isn't he supposed to tell me how *he* feels I've been handling them? "I love doing them with girls instead of the boys' team," I answer honestly, and both coaches laugh. "It's a lot more mileage than I'm used to, but so far I'm feeling pretty good."

This is the answer Coach wanted, I can tell by the way his face relaxes and he eases forward in his chair. "No aches or pains?" he clarifies.

I shake my head, understanding his concern. "No, I think the base mileage I did this summer helped prepare me." Instead of ramping up my mileage all of a sudden, Coach Harding worked with me as soon as I graduated high school to slowly increase the length of my runs without putting my body under too much stress.

"Our annual scrimmage is coming up in a couple of weeks, and I'd like to reevaluate where you're at after that."

"What do you mean?" I wonder. The scrimmage – an odd title for a cross meet – is an unofficial race.

"I don't want to talk specific goals yet. You've still got a lot of adjusting to do, and we need to see how you hold up before putting too many expectations on you."

I can't help a deep frown. I was hoping for more positive feedback than this. He's not telling me anything about my role on this team. I need goals. I need to know what he expects from me. What the team expects. I thought I'd shown over the past few weeks of workouts that I was worthy of being someone who mattered to this team. I might be a freshman, but I want to make a mark on the UC running program.

Coach Harding still isn't sure if I will. Does he think I already reached my peak in high school? Is he wary because of my shin injuries last year?

Susan interrupts my thoughts. "We usually don't talk much about specific season goals with the freshmen until late September. There are so few meets in a college season, and it's hard to tell who will be at those meets this early on."

"You mean I might not race this season?" I don't understand. I've given them no reason to think I might not be ready to race. Seven runners can get points for the team at a meet, and they bring twelve runners to most meets except for the last couple. I'm consistently one of the top seven in the workouts.

"I'm quite confident you'll be one of our top runners at the championship meets, Pepper," Coach Harding reassures me. "You'll find your goals are closely tied with the team's goals and how everyone does. As you pointed out, you're not on your own here like you were at Brockton Public."

"Yeah, okay. So, just keep doing what I'm doing?"

"Keep doing exactly what you're doing." That's all he says. And the meeting's over.

I don't know why I leave feeling confused and disappointed. I wanted something more concrete. Even if he told me I needed to pick it up, that he expected me to be the number one runner and lead the team to Nationals, it would have been better to hear than nothing.

I didn't do a ton of research on college coaches before I came to UC, because I was always pretty sure this is where I'd go to college. Now I'm wondering if Coach Harding has a reputation for having a hands-off approach. It doesn't seem that way, aside from the meeting today. He stayed in close contact with me all summer, and he's always right there at our workouts, watching, calling out splits, encouraging.

He's the kind of person you want to impress, and that's an important attribute for a coach. I want him to trust me too. And I can tell he doesn't yet. Maybe he's afraid I'm too fragile. Maybe he doesn't think I have as much potential as he hoped I would. He was positive but vague about where I stood.

It's unsettling.

The campus is buzzing with energy as I make my way over to Chapman Hall. The first week of classes is over, and though it seems to me like people have been out partying every night already, there's anticipation for the first weekend of the year with the entire student body, not just the athletes, on campus. And most of the athletes don't have games or meets yet. We have a long run tomorrow, but that doesn't seem to be holding back some of my teammates, who tried to get me to join them going out tonight. I haven't decided yet. I have more homework than I've ever had before, but it seems like everyone else still has time to get it done and go out, so I don't want to be the odd one out.

I'm surprised to find Chapman Hall almost empty when I arrive. Glancing at my watch, I realize it's almost eight, and the cafeteria is about to close. My teammates have already left, and I manage to scrounge a decent meal from what's left at the salad bar.

I'm eating alone, and feeling a little depressed about it, when Gina places a tray across from mine.

"Hi," she says in her no-nonsense voice.

"Hey, you're running late from practice too, huh?"

She shrugs. "Stayed to do a few drills."

Drills? I'm about to ask more when I notice the salad on her plate. It's full of vegetables but has no cheese, bacon, or croutons. None of the good stuff. Most noticeable, though, it has no dressing. I know there were slim pickings because most of the food has been put away already. But it's weird, for sure – I mean really, a salad without dressing? Yuck.

Before she can register me scrutinizing her plate, I ask, "Are you going out with the team tonight?"

She nods. "Yeah, we all try to get our partying in before the season picks up, you know? Because once we're racing and traveling, we hardly have time to keep up with schoolwork."

"Makes sense," I agree, knowing Jace's team follows a similar approach.

I notice her watching something over my shoulder and I glance behind me. Clayton Dennison is walking toward us, flashing a smile which is surely responsible for catching Gina's attention.

"Hi ladies," he greets us smoothly before sliding in beside me. "Have we met?" he asks Gina.

She shakes her head and introduces herself in an uncharacteristically quiet voice.

"I'm Clayton. Pepper and I went to the same high school," he explains. "Are you all coming to my party tonight?"

"You're having a party?" I ask.

Before he can respond, Gina says, "Yeah, I think a bunch of us were going to head over there later. You're at the old Sig Beta house now, right?"

"Yeah. The former frat brothers are doing all the organizing and shit, but it's our place now, so they're just helping us out."

It's news to me that the baseball team took over the fraternity house. If my teammates plan to party there tonight, I'm probably better off staying in and getting homework done.

My cell phone buzzes from my backpack and I smile when I see who it is.

Jace: Can we go on a date?

Me: Yes, please.

Jace: Second dinner?

Me: Perfect

Jace has been in denial all week that Annie is gone. Or he's convinced himself she's on vacation and will be back soon. I don't know because he hasn't said a thing. And I'm afraid to ask. Cold, angry, hurt Jace sucks. Emotionless remote Jace is even worse. So even though I know the bubble of denial is going to burst at some point here, I'm rolling with it.

When Gina and I get back to our dorm, Lexi and Caroline are already dressed and ready to go out, along with half the cross team. Someone has brought over loads of cheap liquor, and our common area smells like a party has been going on for hours. How this all went down in the short period of time between the tempo run and now is a mystery to me. Most of the girls had their meetings with Coach earlier in the week. Though mine wasn't very long, Coach had three meetings before me that were each over thirty minutes, but the rest of the girls couldn't have been at it for too long if they showered and ate before this. I truly hope they took the time to eat.

Music is blaring and a rowdy side of my teammates is coming out in full force. It's not even nine yet and a few of them are well on their way to wasted. It still perplexes me that some of these girls are the fastest college runners in the nation. It's not what I expected of my college teammates, and I think I like it this way. The excitement in the room is contagious, and by the time I'm changed and back out the door to meet Jace, I'm giddy from the overdose of girl-craziness.

Jace has dressed up for our date, wearing dark jeans and a button-down shirt that's not wrinkled. He's usually in workout clothes or sweats, and I grin when I find him leaning against the hood of his Jeep outside my building. Damn, he looks good. I snap a memory shot of him like this, hands in pockets, gazing up at the sky.

"What are you thinking about?" I ask when I approach, taking his hand in mine.

He tilts his head to the side and regards me like he's seeing me for the first time. "You're like an oasis to me. Do you know that, Pepper Jones?" Jace remains still, letting me hold his hand, when he speaks. The line is borderline cheesy, and Jace doesn't do cheesy. Judging by the earnestness in his voice and written all over his face, he means it. "College is crazy. My friends, my teammates, they're all about fun. I love them, but it's like they're trying to escape on nights like tonight, you know?"

"You would know better than I would," I remind him. It wasn't too long ago he sought refuge in drugs, women, parties.

He nods and looks back up at the sky with a heavy breath. "Yeah, I do know. But that was before I knew what you and I could be. That this could work." He pulls me into him, so my body is nestled between his legs. "And not just *work*, but be better than our friendship. Friendships last, and I didn't want to risk ruining it, but now I know that what we have, it's gonna last too."

"Yeah?"

"It's you, Pep, it always has been. Football is fun and it might be my career someday, but you? You're it for me. Being a quarterback, leading this team, I love that. But after practice, after games, it's you who I need. None of it really matters without you in my life."

I suck in a breath. Jace has never bared it all quite like this before. And seemingly out of the blue. He tells me he loves me, but this is more than love that he's declaring. I'm at a loss for words, and all I can do is get closer, pushing up on my toes and tilting my head to find his lips. And when I do, I feel the weight of that truth slide into me and warm my body, my bones. It's a truth I don't ever want to question. In this embrace, we are home.

That is, until Annie decides to burst Jace's bubble of denial in the worst possible way.

JACE

Pepper's been in the passenger seat of my Jeep thousands of times, but I'll always have trouble keeping my eyes on the road when she's sitting beside me. Her presence is warm and bright and my eyes just can't seem to look anywhere but in her direction when they know she's nearby. And shit, Pepper is beautiful. The kind of beauty that never gets old and never wears off. She has no idea, and that only makes her so much more appealing.

When I got back to my apartment after practice, Pepper was on my mind. Nothing unusual there. I'm always thinking about the next time I'll see her, and wondering what she's doing, how her day is going. It's been that way for as long as I can remember. Sometimes I get this crazy feeling like Pepper might not have any idea how much she matters to me. It seems so obvious from my perspective that I often don't vocalize it. But tonight I really wanted to make sure she gets how it is for me.

When I saw her come out of the building, those long-ass legs trying to distract me from her gorgeous smile as they always do, I fell in love all over again. How many times can you fall in love with the same person? It happens to me every fucking time I see her. I go deeper and deeper and I wonder if there's a bottom or if it will always be like this.

I probably sounded like a lovesick asshole when I started telling her how special she is, but when it comes to Pepper Jones, I always have been a total idiot. And seriously, I tried to tone it down, but once I started saying shit, and she looked so blown away, it all poured out. The girl is my light, my center. Like gravity, she keeps me grounded.

When we get to the restaurant, I run around to the passenger door, eager to have her touching me and at my side. I'm not oblivious to the dudes at the bar checking her out, but she remains clueless as I give them my most intimidating glare. She just leans into me, her happiness pure and transparent. Pepper doesn't play games with me; she's always made her emotions and thoughts perfectly clear. I love that about her.

She's telling me about her teammates throwing a party in her dorm room, and her innocence is endearing. She wants everyone to be happy and safe, and the constant drinking and partying in college gets to her. She worries. It's cute. Her capacity to love amazes me. She already feels it for her new teammates, and I'm sure if one of them called her with a crisis right now, she'd do all she could to fix it.

But it's my phone that rings. The number is unknown, and I'd normally hit the "decline call" button, since it's most likely a reporter, but there's a chance it's Annie, so I accept the call and bring it to my ear.

"Jace? Hi baby, it's your mom."

I don't respond. Her voice is different and I know immediately what that means.

"I'm sorry I haven't been in touch," she says, not sounding sorry at all. "I got your messages, it's just been crazy. Listen, I need your help."

Those words hit me like a hammer straight through my ribcage. Fuck, it's painful. She doesn't care two shits about me. She just needs money. I wait for it. I can't speak as I do. Instead, I throw up the shield I've been working on taking down for years. The instinct to protect myself is just too strong, and I couldn't hold back my armor if I tried. Fucking hammering on my chest is hard to ignore.

"See, an old girlfriend was driving out west and wanted some company. But we were going over the speed limit when we got to California, and she got pulled over. And then she had some drugs in her car, and now we're at the police station."

She pauses, probably waiting for me to ask what I can do to help. Annie doesn't know me at all if she thinks I'm coming to her rescue now. "You're in California?" I ask, just to clarify and to let her know I'm still on the line, though I'm about to hang up. She's going to ask me for money to bail her out, and I want to confirm that she is capable of stooping that low before I shut her out of my life forever.

"Yeah, somewhere in Orange County. Look, the drugs weren't mine. I didn't even know she had them in there."

There's another long pause. She's got about twenty more seconds before I'm done.

"I can't make my bail, do you think I could borrow some money?"

"No. I can't do that."

And that's when I hit the red "end" button. It feels so final, it's almost a relief. The all-too-familiar sense of rejection and self-pity threatens to pierce through me, but there's no way I'm letting it. Instead, a coldness washes over me, and I feel nothing at all.

Pepper's warmth beside me is suddenly suffocating, and I can't bring myself to look at her; the brightness and love always emanating from her is blinding and if my eyes adjust, I'm afraid of what will happen. I'd probably destroy this entire restaurant, and those assholes at the bar who blatantly checked out my girlfriend when we walked in. I don't trust myself with her right now.

If I touch her, talk to her, let myself love on her like I want to, I'll let out the rest of the beast. There's a blackness in me full of anger and resentment and no one wants to be a part of it. It's not something Pepper should ever be exposed to.

So I drop her off at her dorm and seek a distraction. Anything will do.

CHAPTER TEN

The phone call comes in the middle of dinner. Jace wouldn't normally answer a call when he's out with me like this, but I suspect it's her as soon as he glances at the unknown number. He has a frantic look when he answers, and the color in his face drains so quickly as the voice on the other end speaks that I'm afraid he might pass out.

"You're in California?" he asks, his hand gripping the cell tighter with the question.

She speaks for a long time after that, and I hate that I don't know what she's saying. I want to get closer and put my ear next to his, but the wall is there again. He threw it up as soon as the phone rang, and it frightens me that he can do it so easily. One minute we were eating and laughing, and the next he's retreated to a place where he won't let me join him. It was only minutes earlier that he told me I'm it for him, yet in this moment, with his gaze far off, I don't think I'm on his radar at all. His normally tan skin has turned ashen, and I have the sudden urge to smack him in order to bring him back to life. To me.

"No," I hear him say, "I can't do that."

And then he clicks off. He stares at the phone for a long time before speaking.

"An old friend was driving across the country. Annie met up with her and decided to join her for the rest of the drive to California." Jace recites Annie's story in a detached manner. "She called me from the police station. She was arrested for possession."

He won't make eye contact with me when he says all this, and though we're sitting so close our legs touch, he won't let me see or feel any of his emotions. If I had to guess, his heart is breaking in two.

The first sign that he has some reaction to the phone call is when he barks out an ironic, disbelieving laugh. "She asked me to bail her out. She said it wasn't hers. But she was still high on the phone. I could tell."

I reach for him then, trying to embrace him, and though he doesn't push me away, he doesn't let me draw him near either. "I'm sorry, Jace," I whisper. I hate that there's pity in my voice, and I'm sure he hates it more. My heart is breaking too, but for him and what Annie has done.

"She left," he states blandly. "And she's never coming back."

I know what he means. Even if she were to return, she will never again be a part of his life. A part of me is thankful that he has made this decision, that he won't keep hoping and forgiving her, because I fear it would be an endless cycle of heartbreak. Another part of me is afraid for him. Afraid of how this will affect him.

I know what it's like to live without a mom. But right now, I'd rather be in my shoes than Jace's, because I think that having a parent die is easier than having a parent reject you, or choose something else – drugs, at that – over you.

Jace drives me back to the dorm after dinner. He says he needs to be alone right now, and I don't question it. Once again, it hurts that he doesn't seek comfort from me, but I swallow that down and tuck it away. He's told me he needs me in his life, and maybe someday he'll be able to fully embrace those words. For now, his declaration will have to be sufficient.

It's crazy, though, how quickly I find myself questioning the words he spoke, how meaningless they become in the face of his actions. I'm checking my email the next morning, killing a few minutes before heading over to the gym with my roommates. Facebook keeps alerting me about various messages, tags and events, so I reluctantly log on to my account. I've never been a huge fan of Facebook. My friends always got caught up in what was happening on people's Facebook pages, but the internet is not the real world, and I swear some people think it is. The World Wide Web and the real world intermix so much that people get the two realities confused. Gran and Lulu live solidly in the moment (though some might question their grasp on reality) and I want to be like them.

However, I can't ignore the internet entirely, and I check in on my Facebook account to ensure no one's posted a naked photo of me or something. Just some running pics and a few friend requests from teammates. When the screen switches to my newsfeed, a photo of Jace and Frankie laughing flashes before me. It's a great shot, and whoever took it caught them unaware. I click on the photo, and then click on Jace's page, curious to see if there are any other good photos of him on there.

I find about a dozen photos that were posted early this morning – like, at 3:00 – from Instagram. The hashtags tell me that it was the same party my teammates went to, the one hosted by the baseball team. And judging by the shots of him in various locations and taken by several different people, he didn't just stop by for a quick minute. He told me he wanted to be alone when he left me last night, but did he really just want to get away from me?

My stomach twists with the betrayal. He lied to me. This is now the second time he's gone out to party without me. I'm not his keeper, and he doesn't have to bring me with him wherever he goes. But this is different. He's going out without me because he doesn't want me with him. If he wants to forget Annie and the pain she's causing him, I can't fault him for it, but if doing that means ditching me, I can't deny how much that hurts. The small breakfast I ate is churning in my stomach, and I quickly shut my laptop before I feel even sicker.

Working out with my teammates, pushing my muscles on the weight machines until I can barely lift my arms, it helps a little. But when they all decide to go out again that night, I opt to go see Gran at our apartment. Of course, I try to get in touch with Jace, but he's evasive.

Gran's on a date with Wallace the cowboy when I get to the apartment, but when she returns home, she takes one look at me and starts making hot chocolate. When she hands me a mug and takes the seat beside me on the living room couch, I tell her everything. She knows Jace almost as well as I do, and from her expression as I relay the phone call from Monday, she already knows Annie left, relapsed, and got arrested. Gran and Jim are friends, and for all I know, Annie called both of them seeking bail after Jace hung up on her.

"After the phone call, he ended our date, dropped me off at my dorm, and told me he needed to be alone. But he went straight to a huge party on campus, hosted by a guy he doesn't even like," I add, though it's mostly irrelevant to the fact that he lied to me. He wanted to escape being with me. It makes my whole body hurt, an emotional pain that runs deeper than the kind from a hard running workout.

I don't know what I need from Gran right now. I don't want her to get so mama bear on me that she can't give me reliable advice. I guess I need her to do something to take away the pain, to tell me he didn't mean it, that he'll come back to me as soon as he's processed this, and that it won't take long.

"Baby girl, Jace has come a long way in talking 'bout and facing how he feels, but ever since he was little, his first instinct is to push it down and bury it. Anything that hurts, even sometimes the good stuff, if it's too good, he turns the other way. It doesn't take a fancy doc to say it's all 'cause of his mom leavin'. You and me know that good and well."

"But Gran, she left *again*. After coming back and getting to know him. After being sober and making a new life. This time, it's like his dream came true, that she came back and wanted a real relationship with him, and she's smashed it. If he buried how he felt about things before, now what?"

Gran looks truly sad, and I don't know if it's for me, Jace, or both of us. She takes my hands in hers. "I don't know, baby girl. He's come a long way with you by his side. He has. But what Annie did, it's gonna set him back. Real far back. All you can do now is wait. Be patient with him. And if it hurts too much on you, you are gonna need to keep your own heart intact, you hear? He needs a friend right now more than anything, but he ain't gonna admit it." Gran only gets going saying "ain't" when she's fired up or emotional, so I know this news is troubling her.

When one week, and then two go by, and Jace remains closed off, I start to wonder how long I'll need to wait. And should I be doing anything in the meantime? What can I possibly do? I can't force him to heal from this, and pushing him to talk to me will no doubt backfire. I try to remember that he's grieving a loss – it's like his mom died, only worse.

I've seen him only a few times since he received the phone call, and never for very long. We haven't really spent any intentional time together, and there have been no kisses, hand-holding, or hugs, much less sleepovers. But today is my first cross country race as a college student, and my longing for Jace is replaced by excitement and anxiety.

It's not exactly a *race*, just the informal scrimmage against other Colorado colleges, some of which aren't even in our league or division. Still, I'm wearing my UC Brockton uniform and racing on the home course for the first time. The uniform is essentially a bathing suit. The bottoms are called "butt huggers" because they are basically bikini bottoms with slightly more fabric. The tops are skin tight, though fortunately mine does not show my midriff like some do. It's comforting that all of the other girls on the starting line wear the same type of uniform.

When the gun goes off, I move forward with my teammates, trying to stay behind Kiki and Sienna. Coach Harding has given me no advice or instruction. My coach in high school spoke with me before every race about a strategy, expectations and goals. Today, I have none. It should be freeing – I've struggled under pressure before – but instead it's suffocating.

Sienna and Kiki were consistently two of the top five runners on the team last year, and I've managed to stay with them or close behind them on most of our workouts so far. I figure I can treat this like a workout and try to stick with them.

But my body knows this isn't a workout and it's not cooperating. My shoulders and arms are stiff, and my legs refuse to go with the flow. They remain tight and uncertain, and I can't tell if the pace is actually super quick or if it just feels that way because I haven't raced in a while.

Sienna and Kiki surge ahead, and I can't seem to stay behind them.

A swarm of runners moves in front of me as the course narrows, and before I know it, I've lost sight of my team captains. I spot our team colors in front of me and recognize Trish and Gina. With renewed determination, I resolve to stick with these two.

The route winds through a golf course, and my body begins to relax. It's a beautiful September day, and I'm surprised by how many students have come out to cheer. Gran and Lulu are among the fans lining the course, and they are decked out in the school colors. They've also managed to acquire pompoms and are taking great pleasure in pretending to be part of a cheerleading squad when I pass.

The race is one kilometer longer than a high school cross race, which isn't much, but I find I'm happy to have the extra distance when we hit the halfway point. I've been sticking behind a group of girls that includes Gina and Trish, but now that my body is relaxing, I want to pick up the pace.

The freedom of having no expectations but my own hits me, and I realize I don't have to follow anyone through this race. I can run what I feel. And right now, the nerves have transformed to energy and I can't hold back the urgency for speed. Before I know it, I've passed the group, and I'm flying up a short hill effortlessly. Okay, not totally without effort. Breathing is becoming more difficult, but it feels good to push myself. It always has.

There's a gap between the girls I'm pulling away from and another group ahead, where Sienna and Kiki lead the race with three other runners. I hear heavy breathing beside me and glance over to find that Gina has picked up her pace to match mine.

Together, we continue to close in on the lead group. When we catch them, I'm relieved to see there's only one kilometer to go now, because I'm beginning to feel the consequences of picking up my pace, and I'm not sure how long I can maintain it before I hit a wall.

The finish comes into view, and I can feel the group get antsy, wondering who will make a move first. Some girls have a ton of speed and can afford to wait until the last minute to try a sprint for the win. Others, like me, are better off breaking away earlier, because, while I've got a decent kick, my body isn't made for serious sprinting. I can't always hold my own in a dash to the finish with girls at my level.

I'm tempted to make a go for it, but something holds me back. This isn't even a real meet, and I don't want to overdo it. It seems presumptuous, cocky, obnoxious even, that I would even consider trying to win my first college cross race. And that thought causes me to stay in the middle of the pack. A girl from a different team makes a move, and I don't try to go with her. Sienna does, but she's not able to hold on. The girl from Mountain West wins, and I think my official finish is seventh, though we are all very close together.

I'm pleased with the result, but a little disappointed in myself. I don't like that I didn't push for the win at the end. It's like I was afraid I didn't deserve it. No, that's not right. I don't know why I held back, but I won't let it happen again.

CHAPTER ELEVEN

Everyone wants to go out for pizza after the race, but I can't bring myself to join them. I know it's not cool to ditch out on the team like this, but I'm hit with a strong wave of nostalgia, and I find myself alone in my dorm room that night, calling Zoe Burton.

She picks up right away, and hearing her voice puts an instant smile on my face.

"Pepper Jones!" she greets me enthusiastically. "What's up, stranger?"

We've texted quite a bit, but haven't spoken on the phone much since starting college.

"Just missing on you. We raced your school today and a Mountain West girl won," I tell her.

Zoe knows who I'm talking about. Apparently there's a standout on the team at her school. "She actually asked me if I wanted to be on the team when school started, which was like, super weird but kind of flattering."

"Really? You should, you know. Don't you miss it?"

Zoe was a top runner on the Brockton Public team and she'd probably hang in there at Mountain West, if she wanted to. But she laughs.

"I miss *you* but I am having way too much fun to miss training every day."

When she tells me what she's been up to, there's no question that running cross would not fit into her new lifestyle. She's not doing anything that worries me, but she's taking full advantage of the freedom of being away from home and on her own. With a cop for a father, it must be liberating not having to concoct an elaborate scheme every time she goes to a party.

"Charlie and I have been hanging out a lot again," she tells me. They broke up on amiable terms when he went to Mountain West last year, so I'm happy to hear this. "We run together sometimes, actually, which is cool."

The jealousy I feel from her comment is unexpected. I want to run casually with both Zoe and Charlie, like we used to. I miss the ease and comfort of my high school friendships. I also miss that I can't just go for a run whenever I feel like it anymore. Being on a college team is serious business, and all of my runs are dictated by the training program. If I go out on my own, I throw a wrench in that program. I've learned from my own mistakes that extra mileage will only hurt me. Maybe some runners can pull it off, but my legs are doing just fine sticking with the college program.

After chatting for nearly an hour, Zoe has to head out with her friends, who are waiting on her. I hang up feeling like I'm missing out on something. Sure, my teammates are all together and I could be with them right now, but just as I was held back at the race today, something is holding me back from embracing my new team. I loved Brockton Public cross, and it almost feels like I'm cheating on my high school teammates when I get too close to the UC team. It makes no sense, but I just can't bring myself to replace my old team with a new one. It feels disloyal.

Before I know it, I'm texting Jenny Mendoza, asking her what she's up to. Jace is at an away game until tomorrow, and I don't want to be alone right now. She texts back that the team didn't have a race today and the girls just got back from a long run. Though the irony of the situation doesn't escape me when she invites me to pizza with the team, I don't hesitate in accepting.

I'm at Lou's thirty minutes later, and I find Jenny with at least a dozen of our teammates taking up two corner booths. Though Jenny and my old teammates are happy to see me, it takes about five seconds after sliding into a seat before I feel like an intruder. They eagerly ask me about UC, and talk to me about how their season is going so far. But I'm not part of that season anymore, and I shouldn't be here.

I graduated, and I'm now part of the Brockton Public cross team's history. I need to accept that. I get the distinct impression that my old teammates would prefer to talk about me as part of their past than *with* me, at this table. It's nothing personal, but I'm throwing off their dynamic. Jenny is the leader now, and with me here, she's not. It was the same when Charlie graduated. Rollie and Omar became the guys' team leaders. Not to mention, it's awfully strange being here with Jenny and my old teammates, and some newbies, without Zoe. My best friends on the team have graduated.

Before the pizzas arrive, I'm awkwardly excusing myself. I even pretend I got a text message and that I need to be somewhere. Am I imagining it, or does the table breathe a little sigh of relief when I leave? Like, they can go back to normal now?

When I hop on my bike to ride back to campus, I feel more alone then I ever have before.

It's hard to admit, but while Jace grieves the loss of his mother, I'm grieving the loss of high school. It makes me feel so pathetic, and I never realized how hard it would be to let that phase of my life go. Maybe it would be easier if I'd left town, like Zoe. Even after facing the reality that I am no longer a Brockton Public runner, and I'm certainly not betraying them by making UC my new team, I remain reluctant to make new memories. It still feels like by doing so, I'm replacing all the ones I have with Zoe, Charlie, Rollie, Omar, Claire, Jenny, and even Coach Tom.

Lexi's eagerness to include me helps tremendously. It isn't until the following Saturday, though, when I make a real commitment to making new memories. It's the last weekend before our first official meet. We'll be traveling to California for a big invitational. Most girls on the team stayed in on Friday night in anticipation of our long run this morning, but everyone is planning to party hard one last time for the rest of the season tonight. I'm going to go out with everyone, but my heart isn't in it. I'm missing Jace, and I kind of want to curl up in bed and watch a movie and feel sorry for myself. At this point, it's been three weeks since we've had any real substantive time together, and he's avoided my attempts to hang out.

But then I hear the girls talking about the football team's annual party tonight. Jace will definitely be there, I know this because that's where he was last year on my recruit trip. Like us, it's the football team's last hooray before getting serious for the rest of the season.

"A bunch of the football guys were at Alberto's last night," Trish says. "Pepper, I had heard your boyfriend knows how to have a good time, but damn, he was something else!"

I drop my fork. "What? He was at Alberto's?"

She hesitates before answering. "Yeah. With his teammates," she quickly adds, and I know she must register my stricken expression. "You're coming with us tonight, right?"

I nod, a huge lump in my throat preventing me from speaking.

"Yeah, girl," Kiki calls from across the table. "Let's get you out and have some fun!"

Lexi hasn't been the only one trying to get me to check out the college night life. Kiki is a little more hesitant to pressure me, as team captain, but I can tell she thinks I'm taking things too seriously. Maybe she's right. I feel like an idiot. Here I thought Jace was wallowing in grief, and he's out partying. And I realize that he's definitely one of the reasons I've been holding back. It's because I feel guilty. Scratch that. *Felt* guilty. Because I won't anymore. I didn't want to have fun and enjoy myself too much because it didn't seem fair with how much Jace was hurting. That's over now. I'm not exactly livid, more hurt than anything, but it's time for me to live my own life. Jace is doing it and coping how he knows how. I can't sit around waiting for him to come to me.

I know that part of me wanted to stay home in case he needed me. His team is having one of the biggest parties of the year, and he didn't even tell me about it. Okay, maybe I am kind of angry. I let Lexi talk me into to borrowing one of her halter dresses, which is borderline inappropriately short on me, since my legs are longer than hers. And when she offers me a "pregame" shot of tequila, I don't hesitate. Caroline and Gina join us, and Lexi is prepared with salt and lime, showing us how it's done. The liquid hits me in a tangy rush and I clamp my lips around the lime wedge to ease the burn. But the flavor remains on my tongue, and as the liquid warms my insides it emboldens me.

"I think we should do another," I announce.

"Yeah, girl!" Lexi cheers.

Caroline hesitates, but nods in agreement. Gina puts her hands on her hips. "Someone's going to need to watch over you three tonight, so I'll be the responsible roommate."

Lexi throws her arm around me as we walk to the party, "Dude, can we talk about how sexy you look tonight? Your Mr. Wilder is going to want to whisk you away as soon as we get there, but don't let him."

I giggle. I hope he does. It's been too long. "Why shouldn't I let him?"

"Duh!" she exclaims. "Because we're going to get our dance on. You too, Caroline!" she calls to Caroline, who's walking ahead of us. "Tequila gives every girl the ability to shake her booty down."

"Did she just say shake her booty down?" Caroline asks as she slows for us to catch up.

"Or up, whichever you prefer," Lexi says matter-of-factly.

"Sideways?" I ask.

"Just not gently," Lexi explains. "Never shake gently," she warns us.

"Did you take extra shots without us?" Gina asks skeptically from behind us.

"Whoa! Where did you come from?" I ask. I thought she was ahead of us.

Gina rolls her eyes. "I changed my mind. I'm getting drunk with you people. Watching this unfold is entertaining now but you'll be driving me nuts by the end of the night if I stay sober."

"Aha!" Lexi jumps in the air and pumps a fist. After having her arm over my shoulder, her abrupt movement makes me stumble, and then giggle. "I came prepared for this moment," she announces, pulling the tequila bottle out of her giant purse. I wondered why she was carrying such a big bag.

Caroline's eyes widen and she drags Lexi off the sidewalk, into someone's front yard. "We have to hide to drink this!" she tells us in a loud whisper.

I look around. We're probably drawing more attention to ourselves by standing on someone's front lawn like this. Caroline plops down, cross-legged, and pulls Lexi with her. Gina shrugs and joins them on the ground and I follow suit. We're sitting in a circle, like school children, as we pass around the bottle.

For some reason, we keep whispering. People walking along the sidewalk give us odd looks. It doesn't make me question the grin plastered on my face. It's the first time I've witnessed Caroline come out of her shell in a group setting and Gina is letting her guard down. If it takes tequila to get there, I'm okay with that.

By the time we show up at the football house, the party's in full swing. My roommates are looking for the rest of our teammates, but my eyes are seeking out my boyfriend. When I don't find him outside on the lawn, I meander into the house.

A popular song blares, and I find myself humming and swaying my hips as I shimmy my way through the crowd. Boy, Lexi wasn't kidding about tequila bringing out the booty shaking. My hips have a life of their own, but my main mission at the moment is finding my boyfriend. Maybe we can forget all about Annie for the night and just get our dance on together.

The grin I've been wearing widens at this thought as I find my way to the kitchen. I spot the back of Jace's head, his broad shoulders and dark hair drawing me closer. Frankie is leaving the kitchen as I enter, and when he sees me, he doesn't greet me with the smile I expect. If I'm not mistaken, he's cringing.

"Hey, Pepper, how's it going?" he asks.

"It's cool, Frankie, you?"

As he responds, I sense he's trying to draw me out of the kitchen, and I don't like it one bit. Turning away from him, I begin to make a beeline to Jace. I can't wait to jump in his arms, and I hope my enthusiasm to see him will pull him out of his grief. But what I see when I step toward him makes me halt, and the grin on my face drops.

Jace is speaking with a girl. No big deal, there. But it's the way they're standing that cuts off my breath. She's touching his arm, and he's not moving away. She's positioned herself inappropriately close, and he's not giving her any signals to back off. Instead, his head is tilted in her direction, like he's really trying to hear what she has to say over the blaring music. The worst part of it all is that she's not just attractive, she's a bombshell. Stunning. Long legs in tight booty shorts that show off the perfect curve of her waist. Gigantic boobs for such a thin person, and wavy red hair cascades over her shoulders and down her back. She's one of the most beautiful people I've ever seen.

A small part of me wants to walk right over there and make it clear that Jace is taken. But they look intimate and I feel like an intruder, like I shouldn't be here at all. I spin back around, suddenly gasping for air, as I shove my way through the crowds and back outside. My roommates are still out here and they've found other teammates. I'm about to blow right on past them and walk myself home, but when my eyes lock on Lexi, whose eyes show concern even through a drunken haze, I change my mind.

I know I've already had three shots and I'm buzzing, but I reach out for her purse and she hands over the bottle. One more swig, and then I'm done with that bottle for the night. "Shall we get our booty shaking on?" I ask her, pushing down all the emotional turmoil and pain fighting to burst out of me.

"Totally girl, where's the dance floor?" Lexi asks.

Looking around, there's no dance floor. "We'll just have to make one!" I declare. "The music is louder inside, but I like it out here. Let's move the speakers."

Lexi likes my motivation and joins me in my mission to sneak a set of speakers outside. It's not very cloak and dagger, and I notice some of Jace's teammates raising their eyebrows, but no one stops us. We successfully recruit Caroline and Gina to get our dance party going, and it doesn't take long before the entire women's cross team, and a few of the guys too, are getting our groove on on the front lawn of the football house.

I'm letting myself get lost in the beat, not caring how overtly sexy my moves are. Everyone dances like this at college parties, as far as I can tell. Besides, after what I came upon in the kitchen, it was either go home and sob alone or embrace my wild side. My wild side is sort of awesome. I bet the stunning redhead can't dance like I can.

Our dance floor grows, and I happily lose myself in the middle of the crowd, closing my eyes and trying to let my wild side beat down my hurt and lonely side. There's an internal battle going on inside of me, and I'm dancing my way through it. When I open my eyes, I find Clayton Dennison watching me. He's dancing with another girl, but it's not especially intimate. He's not interested in her, even though she's doing her damnedest to get her ass all up in his crotch. I don't even try to suppress the giggle that escapes at her ridiculous antics. No one can hear me anyway.

Clayton's eyes lighten in amusement and he flashes me a smile. My wild side is vindictive and she doesn't mind using someone like Clayton Dennison to win the war against sad Pepper. So I don't look away and when the song ends, Clayton leaves his dance partner and stands behind me. At first, we don't touch as we move, but then his hands settle on my hips and I don't stop him. This is not something a girl with a boyfriend should be doing, but I close my eyes again and let wild Pepper take over.

I don't know how long we dance like this. But after several songs have passed and I open my eyes, the dance floor is still packed. Through the swaying bodies, a flash of shiny red hair catches my eye. I tilt my head to get a better view and what I find sobers me entirely.

She's dancing with Jace. He's looking right at me, and his expression remains impassive when our eyes lock with one another's across the crowded lawn. He looks like he doesn't care. Like none of this matters.

And just like that, my wild side is defeated.

CHAPTER TWELVE

Jace

Melanie's been talking my ear off for longer than I would normally tolerate, but I'm not myself. I've tried not to feel anything, tried to keep myself from drowning in blackness, but it's not working. I throw myself into practice and workouts, and I've even attacked my classes with a ferocity I've never directed at school work before. I go out with my teammates, trying to distract myself from the ache that's always weighing on me, sucking me down, but I don't want to get drunk or flirt with girls. I just want Pepper.

Melanie's apartment is across the hall from ours and she's in my finance class. When she asked to study with me for last week's test, I didn't turn her down. It was another distraction. But I don't want Melanie, and if I don't get rid of her now, she'll get the wrong idea. I'm so fucking tired of trying to stay away from Pepper that I don't have the energy to shake this redhead off. When Frankie nods at me in a gesture that says he has something to say, I welcome the opportunity to detach myself from her.

"What's up, man?" I ask as I approach.

"Pepper's here, dude," he tells me. "What the fuck are you doing with Melanie?" Frankie doesn't hide his disappointment.

I shrug. "Nothing."

"It didn't look like nothing when Pepper walked in and saw her hanging all over you," Frankie points out.

A bolt of panic jolts through me before I can stop it, but I quickly shut down the emotional hurricane before it can take over. After years of practice, I'm the master at controlling not only my outward display of emotion, but I've also got a pretty good handle on what goes on inside. Pepper's always messed with that control, and when she became my girlfriend, I willingly gave some of it up. I can't afford to do that anymore.

Instinct is a powerful thing. Though my instinct is to bury certain emotions, and I'm relying on that right now, I've also got a strong one not to hurt Pepper. To protect her. It sucks when those instincts don't mesh. Right now, they're in a fucking battle.

"Where is she? Is she still here?" I ask, the tremor in my voice giving away some of the war raging inside me.

Frankie shakes his head, and doesn't say anything. He's a terrible liar.

"Tell me, Frankie," I say quietly, and there's no hiding the desperation in my voice now. I crave numbness, but my panic for Pepper is making that impossible.

"She started a dance party outside with Lexi," Frankie says.

It takes less than a minute for me to make my way to the front lawn, where bodies are swaying to a familiar pop song. And when I see her, eyes closed, lost to the music, I know why Frankie wanted to hide her whereabouts from me. She's singing as she moves in perfect rhythm with the music, and Clayton Dennison stands behind her. His hands hold her hips. For a brief moment, all my carefully constructed shields are ripped wide open. I'm raw and exposed. A flood begins to overtake me and I don't realize I'm trembling until someone takes my hand and tugs me forward.

Frantically, I push back the rush of grief, anxiety, sadness, fear, and anger that intermix into a powerful weapon threatening to make me lose control of myself. Of my entire life. My fists clench, ready to fight, but it's not Clayton I'm preparing to go against. It's myself. I've never been so close to letting it all go. It's terrifying. Using all the strength I've built up, I push the ugly down as far as I can, imagining that I'm stomping on it, killing it, until I feel nothing at all. By the time Pepper looks up at me, and I recognize that Melanie has plastered herself against me again, I'm fully protected. Even Pepper can't bring me back now.

CHAPTER THIRTEEN

My head hurts when I wake up in the morning, but I'm happy for the hangover. It's a distraction from the pain in my heart. Because my heart literally hurts. What the hell happened last night? What has happened to my relationship with Jace? I lie in bed, replaying the events, but Jace's blank stare at me as he danced with the stunning redhead is the only image running through my head.

I remember feeling like there were two parts of me fighting each other. The lonely and hurt Pepper and the fun and wild Pepper. But really, it's just one me, and I'm not proud of how I dealt with my emotions last night. Drinking more and letting Clayton dance with me was immature and spiteful. It wasn't a different person doing it. Tequila didn't make someone else take over my body. I knew what I was doing and I wanted to hurt Jace back. It didn't work. Instead, I saw a veil of indifference on him. I don't know if I'll ever be able to break through it.

How could he say all those precious words about needing me in his life only weeks ago and then act like this? I check my phone and find no missed calls or texts. I'm reluctant to get out of bed, and I don't know who else I can talk to about this. My college friends don't know Jace and don't know our history. I find Wes's number and hit call.

His voice is scratchy when he picks up. "Hello?"

"Hi Wes. Sorry, I thought you'd be up. I didn't wake you, did I?" He's two hours ahead in Princeton, New Jersey, so I should be safe, not that I even thought about that before calling.

"Don't worry about it, I need to get up anyway."

"Do you have a minute?" I ask.

"Always, Pep, what's up?"

"Jace was with another girl at a party last night," I tell him.

I hear a sharp intake of breath, and then silence.

"I mean," I clarify, "he was talking to her. Not just talking, but standing close, touching. And she was drop-dead gorgeous, Wes. And then he danced with her."

Wes sighs. "Is there something else going on? There must be something going on."

I probably should have started out by telling him about Annie, but the redhead is the main thing on my mind. I tell him about how she left without a word, Jace flipped out, but then he came around and was fine for a little bit, still thinking she'd return. And then I tell him about the phone call from jail in California.

"After that, Jace just shut down. I've hardly seen him in the three weeks since then."

"Pep, can I tell you what I think he's doing? That's why you called, right?"

"Tell me, Wes." I'm already in so much pain, I don't think what Wes says can hurt much more. Wes is Jace's half-brother – they share the same dad – though to everyone else, they are just close friends. Wes and Jace think a lot alike, and I know Wes will have some insight for me.

"He's pushing you away, Pep. He doesn't want you to leave him like his mom did, so he's controlling what happens. He's trying to make you do it."

I let his words settle. What he's saying is both simple and complicated.

"Wouldn't he just break up with me if he didn't want to get hurt by me? Wouldn't it make sense to hurt me first?"

"No," Wes says firmly. "I don't think Jace has it in him to break up with you directly like that. Instead, he's pushing you, testing your love for him, your commitment to the relationship. He wants to know how strong it is, and if you can't handle it, he wants to know what the breaking point is."

"That's fucked up, Wes." And it's kind of fucked up that Wes sees this. Because even though I don't want to believe him, I know what he says is true.

"Look, he wasn't expecting it with his mom. He didn't see it coming. That's why he's trying to control the situation with you. He can't stand being close to someone now. Hell, he hasn't called me to tell me any of this shit, and we're brothers. I'm hearing about all of it for the first time right now."

"Well, what am I supposed to do? Let him push me away?" I don't think I can do that.

"No. But don't push him to be closer, either. Just hang in there, and show him you're in for the long haul. He can't push you away by dancing with pretty girls. You love him too much to flake out on him for being an asshole."

"Are you telling me I'm supposed to sit here and let my boyfriend treat me like shit?"

Wes is torn by this question, because he knows that's exactly what he's asking me to do. He knows what Jace is doing, and he loves me too and doesn't want me hurt. But he loves Jace more, and he knows that me sticking by him through this is what is best for Jace.

"Did he take the redhead home?" Wes murmurs so quietly I barely register the question. When I do, my heart stops. It didn't even cross my mind that Jace would take it so far. Is it possible he's been with other girls these past three weeks?

I stutter for a moment before responding. "I don't know. I didn't think he could be that cruel."

"I don't think he can be either, Pepper. And I don't think he wants to hurt you so bad you can't even be friends. All I'm saying is, he's testing you, and I hope you'll try to understand it but I know you've got a breaking point. And I don't want you to break. So do what you need to do, but he's hurting bad, Pepper, and he's handling it by trying to avoid feeling anything at all. That means pushing away anyone else who could hurt him."

After we say goodbye, I scream into my pillow for a solid minute. It makes me feel a little better, but I still don't want to leave my room. I spend about an hour lying in bed staring at the ceiling before deciding I need to get out of here and go for a run. I just wish I was still on Shadow Lane so I wouldn't have to see anyone. The odds are high I'll run into a roommate or a teammate.

We don't usually have an organized team practice on Sunday, but Coach Harding expects us to meet up in smaller groups to do an easy run. When Lexi knocks on my door to see if I want to join her and our other roommates for a seven-miler, I'm bummed I didn't sneak out earlier. I'm already dressed and lacing up my running shoes, so it'd be pretty antisocial and weird of me to try to make an excuse to run solo now.

But an idea occurs to me, and I insist that my dog who still lives with Gran could really use some exercise. Though the girls tell me they don't mind running by my apartment to get him, I manage to convince them otherwise and before I know it, I'm jogging up the familiar trail into the foothills with just Dave.

I haven't run alone in weeks, and I need this.

Wes's words ring in my head as I wind my way through trees. This is a test. I get it, but that doesn't make it okay. I may not entirely understand the depth of Jace's pain and anger at his mom's abandonment, but I don't know how far I can let him push me away. And what then? Will he someday see I'm not going anywhere? Will he be ready to heal with me at his side? How long will that take?

The path brings me higher up the foothills but I don't get any answers to my questions. I'm at a point in the trail that I rarely get to, and I know I've probably run a bit too far and pushed myself a little too hard for a day that was meant to be for recovery. But my mind feels slightly more at ease and the turmoil inside me is settling. My heart still hurts, because I know I will have to endure more heartbreak before I have any answers.

When I picked up Dave at the apartment, I promised Gran I'd stay for brunch when I came back after my run. I'm looking forward to a shower, too, as the water pressure in our bathroom is perfect – not too hard and not too soft. I never thought I'd appreciate something like that before living in the dorms and showering there and the locker rooms every day.

Instead of trotting beside me when we enter the apartment building, Dave shoots up the stairs like he's being chased by a bear. Gran must be cooking bacon, because that's the only smell that drives him crazy like this. But as I get closer to the door, where I find Dave pawing at it frantically, the burning smell has me sprinting the rest of the way down the hall. It could be coming from any of our neighbors' kitchens, but Dave's bizarre whining tells me otherwise.

I swing the door open, and sure enough, a cloud of smoke is billowing out of the oven. Quickly, I turn it off, while calling out for Gran.

"Pepper!" she calls from down the hall, and her voice sounds weak and scared. Gran has never sounded weak *or* scared before.

I find her lying on her side in the bathroom.

"Gran!" I rush to her side. Her face is pale, and her fingers shake as she takes my hand.

"I fell, honey. Slipped on some water and banged myself up real good. I can't get up."

"Oh, Gran. Where does it hurt?"

She laughs softly. "Everywhere, but it's my hip that took the hit. I tried to pull myself over to a phone but I knew you'd be back soon. Burnt the quiche. Sorry about that."

"One sec," I tell her before hopping up and running around the apartment opening windows. The last thing we need is the fire alarm going off.

I'm on the phone and calling an ambulance a moment later, and I try to stay composed as she's loaded onto a stretcher and questions are fired at both of us. I hold her hand as we drive to the hospital, and it takes all my self-control not to cry. Gran lying on the bathroom floor, looking so frail and weak on the gurney now in front of me, it's terrifying. What if I hadn't stopped by today? The apartment could have burned down and Gran wouldn't have been able to escape.

I squeeze her hand tighter and tell her over and over that I love her like crazy and please don't fall ever again.

Eventually I have to pry my hand out of hers when we get to the hospital and they take her into a room. I'm still sticky with sweat from the run, and I don't have any way to contact my roommates because I left my phone somewhere in the apartment in the midst of finding Gran and getting her to the hospital. My roommates probably aren't worried about where I am yet, but it sucks being alone right now, and I wish Jace was by my side.

His is one number I have memorized and I'm able to call him from the hospital's front desk. When it goes to voicemail, I fill him in on what's happened.

It feels like hours sitting alone waiting before they call me in. The doctor keeps referring to her full name – Bernadette – when he explains that she has a hip fracture. When Gran doesn't interrupt immediately to correct him, I do it for her.

"It's actually Bunny. Her name. You can call her Bunny."

The doctor raises his eyebrows but nods before continuing. Gran squeezes my hand, thankful. She's too overwhelmed to speak for herself right now, and that scares me too. Gran's a tough cookie and she's frazzled. That truth is doing strange things to me. The fear of losing her and what that would feel like creeps into my heart. It's a lurking dark monster and if it bit I think it would suck me into a black hole that I may never escape.

If Jace is feeling any of that from Annie's abandonment, his need for self-preservation doesn't seem so ludicrous. I think our hearts only have the capacity to handle so much loss before we break. I've never given Jace any sign I'd abandon him though, and I think that's why I can't completely understand what he's afraid of.

CHAPTER FOURTEEN

When I leave the hospital later that night, I find Jace sitting by himself in the waiting room. He's wearing sweats and a tee shirt and there are dark circles beneath his eyes. It's not very late, so the sleep deprivation must be from last night. My stomach lurches at that thought. Does he have it in him to cheat on me? Could he go through with something like that just to push me away?

He's here, though, and that counts for something.

"How is she?" he asks, standing up to meet me.

"Fractured hip. She'll be here for a few days and then she'll need assistance for a while at home, so I'll be staying with her."

"Can I see her?" he asks.

"She's sleeping."

He nods. "Okay."

"Do you want to go back to the apartment with me? I'm going to shower and change, feed Dave, and come back to bring some stuff to Gran. She might be awake by then." I'm angry with him but maybe we can put all that behind us for now, for tonight at least. I need his support right now. Someone who loves Gran like I do should be here with me.

He comes with me back to the apartment and neither of us says much. When he smells the burning, I tell him what happened and how I found her. He looks like he might be sick. Jace doesn't offer a hug or hold my hand. We don't touch at all. I'm so emotionally exhausted at this point that the pain from his continued stand-off hardly registers.

Gran's still asleep when we return to her room later that night. We sit in the two chairs beside her bed, watching her and listening to the monitors.

Finally, I ask the question. "What happened with the redhead last night?" I can't bring myself to be any more direct that that. I would ask *did you take her home* or *did you hook up*, but it's hard to say those words.

"Nothing. I followed you back to your dorm when you left, to make sure you made it okay, and then I went back to my place."

My eyes drop to my feet, and I suddenly feel ashamed. Did I overreact when I saw him talking to that girl? "I'm sorry I danced with Clayton Dennison, Jace."

He clears his throat. "I'm sorry I danced with Melanie."

I wish he hadn't said her name, made her real. It'd be better if he never learned her name, or didn't remember it. "Are we going to be okay?" I wonder.

He doesn't answer at first and I turn to look at him. "Can I spend the night with you tonight?" he asks softly. There's apology, regret, and hope in his voice, and I hope this means he's ready to open up again. That he's no longer trying to push me away. A part of me feared that seeing Gran like this would make him push me away even harder. Because I felt tonight the fear of losing someone, and now I understand just how powerful that fear is. But it sounds like instead of running away from that fear, he's going to face it with me. Despite where we are right now, with Gran's monitor beeping steadily as a reminder, my mouth curves into a small smile and I take his hand in mine, lacing our fingers together.

"Let's stay on Shadow Lane," I tell him.

He nods in agreement, and when we're alone in my bedroom on Shadow Lane that night, he's anything but distant. The opposite of indifferent. He touches me like he's memorizing all my angles and curves. Like it's been ages instead of weeks since he's been with me like this. His lips cover every inch of skin, and his eyes bore into mine when he finally gives in to his release.

The only thing missing is words. I understand if he's not ready to talk yet. There's a lot to say, and my own feelings are jumbled and far too ripe for productive conversation. For now, I just take comfort in his presence. He's come back to me, and I need him now more than ever.

Jace isn't next to me when I wake the next morning. I know he probably had an early practice and needed to get back to his apartment to change before class, but I'm disappointed. Gran will be okay, I know this, but she really freaked me out yesterday, and it's going to be hard to go back to normal life today. I'd rather stay by her side at the hospital, but Lulu is already in Gran's kitchen this morning, insisting on taking over that duty.

"Buns does not want you skipping classes and practices, Salty. She called me yesterday. This is what old lady BFFs are for."

Lulu is on a mission to be Gran's personal assistant. She's cleaned up the burnt mess that I couldn't bring myself to deal with last night, and has been gathering all of Gran's favorite snacks from the cupboards.

"Wallace wants to come by today to see her, and she wants to get out of her hospital gown for the visit. Did you bring her polka-dotted jumper? She looks real nice in it."

Smiling, I assure her that the velvet polka-dotted jumper is in the bag I packed for Gran last night. The top of the jumper looks like overalls but it has a skirt instead of pants for the legs, and I hope it fits loosely over her bad hip. Like Lulu, I know that Gran always feels extra snazzy when she wears it. Everyone has their special outfit, I guess.

It's a busy day. Between explaining the Gran situation to my roommates and getting to classes and practice between a breakfast and lunchtime visit to Gran, I don't have time to worry about Jace's lack of communication until I'm back in my dorm room later that night.

I call Gran, who tells me she's really enjoying the hospital, which makes me laugh. She's making friends with the nurses and docs, and loves how she gets to drink everything from a straw. After telling her goodnight, I dive into my school work for a couple of hours, trying desperately to ignore the fact that Jace has not called or stopped by. I texted him with updates about Gran all day, and he responded with short and minimal messages. He's never been a big texter.

But when the rest of the week goes by without any changes, I know what's happened. He wasn't coming back to me when we spent the night together on Shadow Lane. He was saying goodbye.

This reality doesn't hit me until the day before I fly to my first real college meet in California. Two years ago, I flew on a plane for the first time to California for the high school National Championship. Jace surprised me by showing up to watch. He took a risk with me back then, and it was the best thing for both of us. Am I still a risk for him? Why is he shutting me out when I've shown no signs of leaving?

Gran's discharged from the hospital, and I help her get settled back at the apartment. From the hospital, she apparently assigned Lulu the task of making "travel goodie bags" for all the girls on my team, each bag containing enough sweets to keep us sustained for weeks.

"Gran, we're only going to be gone for twenty-four hours, and we're not going to the desert. I'm pretty sure they have food in California."

Gran just gives me sass about how we're all too skinny. She's back to her normal spiffy self, even though she's stuck with a walker and dependent on others for help.

Like Jim, who is on his way up the stairs to the apartment as I leave, takeout in his hand.

He looks sheepish when I ask if he's brought dinner. "You know I can't cook like your Gran, but she's always liked Chinese, right?"

"Good call, Jim. That's one thing she doesn't cook herself," I reassure him.

We catch up on the usual stuff for a few minutes, but I can't let him go in just yet. "I've actually been meaning to talk to you about Jace," I tell him.

He puts the bag of food down and gestures for me to join him sitting on the steps. "I'm worried about him, Pepper. He's busy and I don't see him a lot, so I can't get a read on how he's dealing with Annie leaving."

"He's been distant," I say hesitantly. It seems we're both looking for information from one another, and neither of us has much to offer. Does Jace confide in anyone?

"With you?" Jim's surprise comforts me.

"I hardly see him anymore, Jim," I admit.

Jim closes his eyes briefly, clearly distressed by this news. "You know, I've always thought as long as you were in his life he'd be okay. You're so good for him, Pepper."

My heart sinks. Jim's concern for Jace is entirely different from my own, which is wrapped up in heartbreak. But the truth is, neither of us can help when he's closed out the world like this.

"What am I supposed to do?" I whisper.

Jim shakes his head, at a loss. "Not much you can do when Jace makes up his mind about something. But don't give up on him, Pepper."

That's three people who have essentially told me the same thing in different words. Jace is going to push me away and I've got to resist. But it's tiring. And I'm getting sick of waiting.

I resolve to confront him when we return from this trip. I've given him a month to cope, and I'm out of patience. I miss him. If I'm supposed to dive into college and leave high school behind, I need him at my side. He's a part of both my past and my present, and I want him in my future too.

I've never been so intimidated by other runners in my life. As we jog through the course before the race starts, I take in the other teams. Every single girl racing here looks like she was designed to run. Fast. Thin and muscular, with determination written all each face. I thought I had a lot of racing experience, but here amongst some of the best runners in the nation, I feel insignificant.

Again, I wish I knew where I stood. Without a sense of purpose on this team or a feel for where I rank amongst my competition, I'm left untethered, drifting. I latch onto that sense of freedom I had when I just ran my own race at the scrimmage two weeks ago. Maybe I need to stop thinking so much and just go by feel. Instinct.

And when the gun goes off, I chant the motto, *don't think, don't think*, over and over again in my head until it fades away and becomes truth.

My fears for Gran, my worry and hurt about Jace, my uncertainty about college running, it floats away as I sprint my way through the throngs of competitors to the front of the group. This is what I always did in a big race in high school, and it's what I'll do now. Running with the lead group is familiar and comfortable, so I roll with it.

The pace is fast, maybe faster than I can handle for six kilometers, but I don't overanalyze it. I just go. I run to set free all the negative energy weighing me down. The more my chest and legs struggle with the pace, the stronger the sense of liberation. A jolt of levity soars through me and reenergizes my muscles, making me go even faster.

When I finish tenth overall, and first for my team, I'm blown away. I'm confident and I know I'm fast, but these are some of the best runners in the country, in the world even. Some of the top runners from Ethiopia and Kenya go to colleges in the states, and I raced them today.

I didn't just hold my own. I rocked it.

Despite the ache and uncertainty haunting me where Jace is concerned, I'm riding a wave of exhilaration as my teammates join me after the race, patting me on the back and recapping their own races. Even Kiki and Sienna, seniors and team captains, seem joyful to have been bested by their freshman teammate. My finish today puts UC on the map. When people talk about contenders for the national championship, we might make the list. The goal to simply qualify for Nationals seems far too easy now, and I have little doubt Coach Harding will be revising the women's team's goals soon.

I've never felt such a part of a team before. Most girls on the team raced well, some didn't, but we placed third overall, which is way better than we expected in this field of top teams. And that's the main thing everyone rejoices in as we head back to the hotel for showers before catching a flight back to Colorado. Home.

The team is officially "dry" for the rest of the season, meaning no drinking. Before I became a college student, it never would have occurred to me that athletes competing at this level would need to institute a team rule to hold everyone accountable for the season. Now that I've seen just how rampant and commonplace binge drinking is every night (and especially on weekends), it makes sense. Not joining in the festivities is defying the natural order of things, and to do that, it takes team solidarity, at least for most of us.

When we get back to campus, the thrill of racing in the first big meet of the season has taken its toll, and we're all exhausted. Partying isn't even on our radar as we say our goodbyes, make plans to meet for recovery runs tomorrow, and head our own ways. I'm not going back to my dorm though. I have somewhere else I need to go.

I texted Jace and tried calling him earlier, and he hasn't responded. That doesn't stop me from walking straight to his apartment, still carrying a giant duffel bag from the trip. I'm not going to sit around and let him push me away like this anymore. It's too painful, and we've been best friends for far too long for him to treat me like this. He's come so far since we've been more than friends too, and letting him treat me like this isn't going to help him or our relationship.

Taking a deep breath, I knock on his door, and Frankie answers a moment later. He's barefoot and wearing sweats, clearly having no intention of going anywhere tonight. The football team might not initiate a "dry" policy, but after their last hooray last weekend, most of them will lie low for the rest of the season.

"Hi, Frankie. Good game today." He knows why I'm here, and he lets me in.

"Thanks. How was your meet in Cali?"

"Great. Awesome, actually." I glance around the small apartment as I respond, and find no sign of Jace. His bedroom door is open, but he's not inside.

"Jace went out, Pep. I'm not sure where, but you're welcome to hang here, if you want," he offers. Frankie's always been friendly, but there's the distinct sound of pity in his voice tonight, and it makes me nervous. I'm inclined to ask him what's going on, but I have a feeling he doesn't know any more than I do. Besides, I don't want to put him in the position of coming between Jace and me. My heart clenches at the thought that it may come to that.

I hesitate, but decide to take him up on the offer. My only other options are to go back to the dorm or wander around campus looking for Jace, and I've already done both of these things on other occasions without great outcomes. "You sure you don't mind if I stay?"

"Not at all, but..." He pauses, and his cheeks redden. The sight of a 300-pound guy blushing is precious. "A girl is coming over soon."

"A girl, Frankie?" I give him a hard time.

"It's the girl from that night," he admits, and I know he's talking about Lizzie Valentine. "We started seeing each other again recently."

"That's cool," I say and pat him on the back in reassurance. We settle on the couch, absently watching ESPN. Frankie's presence helps, but I'm tied up in knots, wondering where Jace is and what he's doing.

At a commercial Frankie turns to me. "I'm worried about him too, Pepper. Do you know what's going on with him?" he asks, and I realize Frankie has no idea.

"He hasn't said anything?" I don't know why I'm surprised. It just seems like Jace would mention something about it to his roommate. He hadn't told Wes either, which tells me he hasn't spoken about Annie to anyone at all. Maybe Jim, but probably not. I'm pretty sure Jace learned about burying his emotions, to some extent at least, from his father. I really can't imagine them having a heart to heart.

Frankie sighs. "Is it his mom? She hasn't come to watch any practices in a while, and he hasn't mentioned her either."

"What did he tell you about the day he disappeared?" I wonder.

"Just that something happened with his mom. He was apologetic about it but wouldn't tell me any details. And then he seemed fine for a week, so I didn't worry. I thought maybe something was up with you guys because he changed again after a date with you."

I give Frankie a very basic rundown of what happened. Even though it's Jace's business to share his life, it bothers me that Jace has closed out Frankie too. I don't tell Frankie about Annie's history with drugs, or that she already abandoned him once. I just tell him that she moved without really talking to Jace about it beforehand, and he's upset about it.

"And yeah, I guess you were right about something being up with us too. That's why I'm here. He can't avoid me forever."

When Lizzie arrives, we chat awkwardly for a moment before the two of them go into Frankie's bedroom and I find a movie on TV to help pass the time. When it's over, and there's still no sign of Jace, I go into his bedroom. Sitting on his bed, alone, I'm flooded with anxiety. What if he comes home with another girl? What if he's doing drugs again? It terrifies me that I went from trusting him completely only weeks ago, to now, when I'm questioning everything. This time last year, our commitment to each other was tested by outside forces most young couples would never withstand, but our faith in each other remained strong. Now, here I am, staring at his mostly-blank walls, imagining the worst in him.

It doesn't escape my notice that the photo he kept of Annie on his dresser is now gone. He's still got a photo of me, so that's something.

Though I'm tempted to run, to avoid getting hurt more by this boy, I try to remember what Gran and Wes told me: patience. Like Wes said, Jace wants to know if I'll be there for him no matter what, which means I have to be prepared for him to push me away. I just don't know if I can take it. It's different for friends or family. Jace is more than that. He's the love of my life. And he has the ability to break me as much as I do him.

If I let him push me past breaking point, we both lose.

It's three AM when he returns. No girl with him, and he's not drunk. The relief at that has me reaching for him. Longing for him to just hold me. But he remains at the foot of his bed, watching me like I don't belong here.

"What are you doing, Jace?" I ask quietly.

"Shouldn't I be asking you that question?" The harshness in his tone startles me.

"I'm here to talk. I have things to say to you."

He begins to take his shoes off. "Okay, talk then."

His words and their coldness nearly send me running right there and then. I guess he didn't need to cheat on me with girls or drugs to send me away. But I have to say it.

"I'm here, Jace, and I'm not going anywhere. You can't hide from me, from everything, forever, you know."

"What makes you think I'm hiding from anything?" He tugs his shirt off before working on his pants. He's undressing in front of me, and I can't help the desire that tugs at my gut as he does.

"You hardly speak to me. You're avoiding me."

Jace gets in on the side of his bed, in nothing but his boxer briefs now. "I guess it's time for me to do this, then."

"Do what?"

"Look, things were good with us, Pepper. But it's time to enjoy college for what it is. I'm not a relationship guy. I tried and I just don't want to do it anymore."

My throat goes dry as sandpaper. He's not looking at me. He's sitting in bed, staring at his hands, and everything in me wants to believe he's lying.

"That's not true," I whisper.

His eyes dart to mine briefly, and I know mine are filled with tears. "It is. And I'm sorry."

A logical, detached part of me knows what he's doing and knows it's because he's afraid of losing me. He's dumping me before I can dump him. But when he's detached and cold like this, it's hard to think I could affect him at all.

"You're a coward, Jace Wilder." It's all I can get out before I run.

CHAPTER FIFTEEN

I race across the quad, my duffel bag making my gait awkward, but my sobbing gasps are the real thing that makes the couple making out on the sidewalk turn and stare. I'm shattered. No matter the reason for Jace doing this, it's irreversible. We will never be the same again. And as I struggle up the stairs and into my room, I don't think anything I've ever felt hurts this much. The agony is bone deep. My insides, my skin, my stomach, head, and definitely my heart, feel the utter misery of this loss.

It takes a while before I realize I never made it to my bed. I'm curled up in a ball on my floor, and if someone walked in they might think I was shot in the stomach with the way I'm rocking back and forth moaning. It hurts so much.

Words don't mean anything. He's avoided me because he doesn't want me anymore. I can seek reassurance from Wes and Gran that he's emotionally damaged, and it has nothing to do with his love for me. But it doesn't even matter. He'd rather be without me. That's the brutal truth.

And my words only mean so much too. I can tell him I'll always be there for him, but I lied too. Because I can't be there for him now. Not even as a friend. It's all destroyed. And this is why it hurts so much. Because I don't think I can have Jace Wilder in my life at all now.

I gulp for oxygen, but even breathing hurts. I see Jace and me running into each other in ten or twenty years, and finally being healed enough to talk like old acquaintances. We'll have both moved on. Cue another round of sobs.

There's a gentle knock on my door, and Caroline pokes her head inside. Her room is next to mine, and my meltdown must have woken her.

"Hey," she says quietly before sitting beside me. She begins to rub my back in circles, not saying anything. Her presence is soothing, and after a while I stop crying.

Eventually, I sit up, hug her, and climb into bed. She tugs off my sneakers and tucks me in like a small child. I think I sleep a little, but even though the sun has risen when I wake, the world feels very dark.

Out of habit, I change into running clothes. I can't eat my usual banana and granola bar though. My stomach is in knots. When I come out of the bathroom after brushing my teeth, I find Caroline, Gina and Lexi waiting for me in the common area.

"We're going on a run," Lexi declares, taking my hand. "Gina's driving us to her special spot."

I don't respond, just follow her to Gina's car, and stare out the window until we arrive at a trail I've never seen before. I'm not sure how long we drove, but I thought I'd already discovered all the good running trails in and around Brockton.

Apparently not. The four of us jog in silence along a creek, and I'm amazed we see no one else. That's unusual on a beautiful Sunday morning. Eventually we get to a waterfall, and Gina leads the way up a boulder where we settle on top, the spray from the falls almost reaching us. I take my teammates' silence as a sign of solidarity, but the clean air and beauty surrounding me only make me want to cry again. As soon as I stop running and am alone in my head again, the pain of his loss is overwhelming.

I know I have to say something, even though my roommates likely already suspect what's happened. "Jace broke up with me last night," I say on an exhale. The words, and their meaning, unsurprisingly bring a round of tears, which I rapidly wipe away.

Gina speaks first. "We're here for you, Pepper, okay? Whatever you need."

Lexi and Caroline echo that sentiment, and I try really hard not to blubber. Here, on this rock, I know Gina has shared a spot that brings her peace that was hers alone. With all four of us watching the waterfall, a little light flickers in my aching heart. I'm creating new memories right now, even if tainted with the loss of old ones. It's enough to get me through today.

After the run, I know I need to stop by to see Gran. Lulu has designated herself as Gran's live-in nurse and is staying in my room, which gives me some reassurance, but I still want to check in on her myself. There's no way I can hide from her what's happened, though, and I really don't want to talk about it.

Lexi and Caroline offer to come with me this time. Gina has a big project she has to do, but each of my roommates has come with me to visit Gran this week. It's no surprise they enjoy visiting her. Even if she's in no position to be baking and feeding them, she's a hoot.

The last thing I expect when I get there is to discover that Gran already heard about Jace breaking up with me from the boy himself. He hasn't seen her since the hospital visit, but has been calling every day to check in. Even though it makes me angry beyond belief that he hasn't shown up in person, a small evil part of me finds it reassuring that I'm not the only one he's treating badly. No matter what, though, it's impossible not to take his break-up personally. People can tell me all day that it's because of Annie and Jace's issues, but in the end, he didn't want me.

I'm expecting Gran to give me a spiel about just that – how it's him not me – but she surprises me when she doesn't talk about it all. She just hugs me. Hard. For such a small little lady, she can sure give a bear hug. It feels so good, and in that hug, I think she reaches in and takes away some of my pain.

"Are you two pretty little ladies gonna help me take care of my granddaughter?" she asks Lexi and Caroline.

"Gran," I start to scold her.

"Because," she interrupts me, "she's gonna need some watchin' out for, you know." Gran continues to go on about friendship, and Lulu pipes in with her own two cents. Caroline and Lexi sit in rapt attention, soaking in their words like they are gold.

As the days go by, I know my roommates aren't just checking up on me because Gran asked them to. I'm grateful they are there to keep me going, but sometimes I wish they'd go away so I can just immerse myself in grief. It's weird that I crave that, but I need to replay all my memories with Jace all over again, through this new lens. Have I always been blind when it comes to Jace Wilder?

There's a hope I can't squash that he will show up at my door begging my forgiveness. I've already imagined what I'll say, how it will all go down. But as the days turn into weeks, and Jace doesn't come back to say he messed up, that he didn't mean it, that he was just hurting, I start to wonder if he has all of us fooled. Did I ever know him like I thought I did? His ability to shut me out like I don't even matter frightens me. It makes me afraid of him and for him. Does anyone really know Jace Wilder?

I see him once in a while, from a distance. He's bold and hard to miss. The way he holds himself, leads his teammates on and off the field, it draws people to him, puts him on a pedestal I don't think he deserves anymore. He interests me, fascinates me, but I don't have him figured out. I don't think I ever did.

It comforts me that he's still in my orbit. That he hasn't disappeared entirely, even if we never speak. But as the weeks tick on and he remains aloof, I find it increasingly difficult to stay away. This can't be how we end. He can't really want me out of his life. It's been a month since he told me it was over, but I haven't entirely accepted it. I've been certain he'll regret it, realize it was a mistake he made in the midst of losing Annie, and we would hash it out and try to get back on track.

I told him I'd always be there for him, and even though it hurts my pride to do it, I've got to show him I meant what I said. That's what I'm telling myself when I knock on his door one Thursday evening. We are both traveling out of state this weekend for competitions, and I can't wait another day to talk to him.

He answers my knock, and I immediately struggle to breathe at the sight of him. He's wearing athletic shorts, and that's it. No shoes or shirt. There's a pen behind his ear, which I find adorable. His jet black hair is a little longer and though it still flips up at the top without any styling on his part, the sides have grown out, giving him a bedhead that makes me want to reach up and run my fingers through. But I don't have a right to do that anymore.

He stands there, the door partially open, not inviting me in. He doesn't say anything. Not even hello.

"Can we talk?" I ask, cringing at the timidity in my voice.

"I'm busy right now," he says in a soft, pleading voice. He wants me to leave, but he doesn't want to hurt me any more than he has. And yet, that's the most painful thing of all. "I'm studying for a midterm," he offers.

Studying has never stopped Jace from having a conversation, and I can't decide whether to accept his excuse. I came here to force him to face me, and I'd be naïve to think he'd make it easy. With determination, I take a step inside. "You can take a quick break."

But when I turn to go to the couch, I find the redhead sitting there. Melanie. I haven't forgotten her name. Yes, there are books and papers strewn on the coffee table and floor, but she looks entirely too comfortable sitting there in a tank top and thin pajama bottoms. Like she lives here or something.

My eyes burn with the effort not to cry as I spin around and awkwardly try to get around Jace and through the door. I'm reminded that he's barely dressed as I nearly collide with that familiar chest and abs. He seems to hesitate, like he wants to stop me, but instead he moves to the side, allowing me to pass. I can't look at him.

Once again, I'm walking back from Jace's apartment in tears. This time, I know it's over. Really over. It doesn't hurt as much. The anger helps. I focus on the anger, resolved not to shed another tear over this boy. It's a resolve I'm quite certain is impossible, but I'm going to try anyway.

Gran's rehab, my new teammates, school, running, these are the things that matter now. Jace has made it quite clear he doesn't want me interfering in his life, and no matter his reasons, it's time I accept it.

The last thing I expect when I get back to my dorm is an intervention. Lexi and Caroline are sitting in the common area with Sienna and Kiki, and I can tell they've been waiting on me when I arrive and they all look at me expectantly.

"What's going on?" I ask curiously.

"We're worried about you and want to talk," Kiki says.

The rage directed at Jace is masking nearly every other emotion as I sit down in one of the armchairs.

"Pepper," Sienna begins, "we know you've been through a lot since college started, with your Gran and Jace," she adds, like I might not understand what she means. "But we're worried about how you're coping."

"What do you mean?" I interrupt. Seriously, I don't get it. Running is the only thing going right in my life, so what's the problem?

"We've noticed you've been skipping meals a lot lately," Kiki says. "And not to beat around the bush, but you've lost weight you didn't have to lose in the first place."

What the hell? I glare at Lexi. "Did you put them up to this?" I ask her, finding a new target for my anger. "Do you accuse everyone of having an eating disorder? Maybe you're the one we should be worried about!" I'm standing now, fists clenched. She stands too.

"Actually, I'm the one who told them you're just upset, and we shouldn't make it into something it's not."

I huff, unsure where to direct my anger now. It's Caroline who speaks up next. "All we're saying, Pepper, is you need to take care of yourself. Losing so much weight this fast is only going to make you sick or you'll get injured. You're running really well, but part of it is because of the weight loss." She takes a deep breath before continuing. "Not to be mean, but running fast from rapid weight loss doesn't last. It's temporary. What lasts is the damage to your body."

Whoa. Caroline rarely speaks boldly like this in front of others, and her words send me back down to the chair.

Caroline continues in a clear and quiet voice, "Believe me, that happened to me when my dad died and I had the best running season of my life, followed by stress fractures and a year of recovery."

I look at the four faces around me, seeing nothing but concern and anxiety. And it's all for me. After all the stress I've felt for Jace and his problems, it's nice to have others worry about me. And I don't want to let them down by my inability to cope. I won't be like him.

"Look, the main reason I've been avoiding meals is because it's really hard for me to see him, and his team is usually at Chapman Hall at the same time as us." I don't tell them I just came from his apartment. I'll sound pathetic. I *feel* kind of pathetic. But despite how upset I was a minute ago by the suggestion I have something more serious than heartbreak and stress over Gran going on, I'm actually feeling a turnaround happening here. I'm not sorry I went to Jace's because it gave me closure. A month ago, the very idea that there was such a thing as closure between us would have killed me, but now at least I have answers. I'm not sitting around hoping for something that will never happen.

"Now that I know things are really over with him, I'm a little more prepared in terms of knowing how to act."

"What do you mean?" Lexi asks.

"I know I should just ignore him. That's what he wants." I can't explain the whole story to them, but the truth is, I couldn't bring myself to treat him any differently until now. It would be like accepting that we're over. Now I know for sure that we are. Over.

"I'm glad you'll start joining us for team dinners, Pepper, we've missed you," Sienna says. "Will you eat something maybe, too?" she asks with a smile.

"My stomach has been in knots, and honestly, I just haven't been hungry. So far it hasn't really impacted my running, but you're right, I can't keep it up. I'll try harder," I promise. And I will. Now that I know how bad it's gotten, that my team captains and roommates are concerned, I know I need to really try to take care of myself.

The five of us stay up chatting for a while after that. It seems each of them has a bad breakup story of their own, or knows one about someone else, and I find myself laughing for the first time in weeks. It's hard, though, because this feels like so much more than just another bad breakup.

CHAPTER SIXTEEN

Jace

Watching Pepper rush out of my apartment building, knowing I've hurt her, *again*, is fucking torture. But when the rage overtakes me, I'm filled with hot anger, directed at myself mostly. My fist is already through the door frame before I realize what I've done.

"Fuck!" I growl. Gathering myself, I turn to Melanie. "Can you leave? We're done studying." Being an asshole to this girl is not something I care about right now. I need her gone. She knew well enough what she was getting into when she started hanging around me while I still had a girlfriend. I've had to push her advances off more than once, but she keeps coming over to study for tests in our finance class, and it's easier sometimes to let her than to get her to go away. Totally regretting not giving her the boot sooner now, though. I don't even want to think about what Pepper thinks she saw. I'd just pulled off my shirt to change after spilling coffee on it when she knocked. If only I'd taken two damn seconds to pull another one on. But no, this will push Pepper away, and that's the right thing to do.

I can sense Melanie lingering, wanting to approach me, so I make my point clear by going into my bedroom and slamming the door. The thud is satisfying but my hand twitches, wanting to pound on something again. Knowing I can't mess with my throwing hand, I check my phone to see who's texted me about what's going on tonight. As soon as I hear the front door close, I pull on a sweatshirt and shove my feet in some shoes before grabbing my wallet and heading outside.

First, I jog in the direction of Pepper's dorm. I don't expect her to still be out, but I'm disappointed not to see her. I've been such a fucking creeper lately following her around at a distance. This time, I just stand for a moment outside, gazing at her window, wondering what she's doing. But if I stand too long, my mind starts to think too hard about things I can't think about, so after a moment, I head to the bars.

Alcohol and women still don't appeal to me. I'll have a drink or two, but mostly I go out to avoid being alone in my head. Kicking ass in football and class is easy when I'm desperately trying to escape being alone with myself. Because I really hate myself, almost as much as I hate Annie for making me such a fucking hateful guy. Football and school aren't always enough, and when they fail me, I surround myself with people.

What matters is that I've still got my thoughts and emotions under wraps. The only person who can make my control slip is Pepper, and that's why I've got to stay away.

PEPPER

Fury is my middle name this week. It's the engine that gets me through each day. I'm red-hot with it, and it's directed at one extraordinarily attractive dark-haired guy, who had the audacity to move on like I meant nothing to him. For all I know, he was with this Melanie girl before he officially broke up with me. I don't even mind thinking these horrible thoughts about him because it adds fuel to my engine of anger.

The championship season is in full force, and it's crazy how it snuck up on me. In high school, it seemed like I was waiting forever to get to the important meets. The UC cross schedule consists of the scrimmage in September, two big invitationals in October, the Conference Championship and then the Regional Championship in November, and finally Nationals in December. Unless the entire team comes down with the flu or something, the assumption is that the team (at least the top seven) is going to Nationals. Knowing that Nationals is more or less a guaranteed thing is incredibly helpful in terms of training. The past two seasons, I didn't know when my season might be over.

I've been the top runner on the team at the last two invitationals, but I still don't put any pressure on myself to repeat that feat at the conference meet today. Unlike at Brockton Public, all five of the top runners on the team could beat one another on any given day. At practice, we're right by each other's sides, and Kiki, Sienna, Trish and Gina have been less than a minute behind me at the last two meets.

Lexi and Caroline have traded off for sixth and seventh place, and I know they are feeling the pressure to hold their places on the lineup today. This is the last meet that allows twelve runners per team, and Coach will have to make a call about which seven runners go on to Regionals. If Lexi and Caroline are six and seven again, the decision will be easy. Another freshman, Wren Jackson, occasionally keeps up with the top group at workouts, but none of our other teammates have placed in the top seven on the team at a race this season. Still, anything can happen at a cross race.

I've managed to channel all my bitterness toward Jace into my legs, and I'm in the lead when we head into the final mile. There are several other runners breathing down my neck as the realization that I might just win the Conference Championship hits me. With it, my legs remind me that I've just let loose with no regard for pacing or restraint for several miles, and the finish is nowhere in sight. My quads contract, signaling that I'm near my limit.

Reluctantly, I give in to my screaming muscles, acknowledging that I can't run on emotions alone, although it sure is fun to try. I gave it my best shot, but if I want to finish this race with any dignity, it's time to simmer down fiery Pepper before I go down in flames.

Letting the girls behind me take over, I settle in behind them, recognizing two of my teammates in the group. With three of us up front like this, we've got a shot at taking the team championship, even if the rest of the team is farther back. With one kilometer to go, Gina pulls away from the group, and another runner stays at her shoulder.

I'm sucking in oxygen, doing all I can to hold on as the group begins to break up, some picking it up to sprint to the finish, while a couple, including myself, struggle to maintain this pace. A few runners come up from behind and pass us, which is the worst feeling ever, but there's really nothing I can do to go any faster. I'm not all that disappointed when I cross the finish line in fourteenth place. I really didn't feel like I had a choice but to approach this race like I did – all in. If I'd given in to any other emotion aside from anger, I'd probably still be at the starting line, curled up in a ball.

I'm still not sure if Gina pulled off the win or got second place, so I look around the finish area for her. Either way, congratulations are in order. She's past the crowds, hands on hips, watching the rest of the runners pull through the finish line. Even from a distance, the greyish hue of her skin gives me goosebumps. Most of the other runners are flushed and rosy from the exertion, but not Gina. As I near her, I notice she's swaying ever so slightly, like it's taking all of her energy to stay on two feet.

When I reach her and touch her shoulder to ask if she's all right, her skin is cold and clammy. "Gina?"

She blinks several times. "Hey, Pepper, I don't feel so good. I'm going to sit down." When she stumbles, I catch her and help her to the ground.

Kiki joins us, and we exchange worried glances. "I'll go see if someone from the medical tent can come over here," I murmur before running toward the white tent I spotted earlier. I'm back a moment later with a medic, who begins examining Gina and asking questions.

This isn't anything I've witnessed at a running race before. I've see girls puke, faint, collapse, and even pee themselves, but Gina's condition scares me because it's so bizarre. I don't know how anyone can be cold after running so fast, especially because it's fairly warm out. The Conference meet is in Arizona, and even though it's early November, there are no signs here that winter is coming. It's already snowed a few times in Brockton.

While Gina is brought to the medical tent, Sienna and Kiki lead the rest of us in a cool down. Caroline and Lexi finished in the top seven on our team again, and I'm relieved that they will both be continuing on with the final two meets. Based on how well the top five did today, I'm assuming we took the win, but the team remains sedate as we silently jog around a field near the course. We're all worried about Gina, and it doesn't feel right to celebrate without her, especially since she led the team today.

Lexi accompanies me to the restrooms while the rest of the girls cheer on the guys' team. I can tell she's champing at the bit to get me alone. She didn't see Gina before she went to the medical tent, and she grills me on what happened. I don't have much to tell her.

"Didn't you wonder why Gina was the only one who wasn't at that little pow-wow last week?" she asks when I've finished describing Gina's condition.

"You mean the one where you all told me to eat more?" I try to sound amused, like it was no big deal.

"Yeah, and don't be a smartass. It wasn't just about that, and you know we were right. You've been eating like a horse all week since we brought it to your attention."

I laugh. It's true. I still don't have my usual appetite, but it bothers me that my problems caused so much concern, and I don't want them worrying about me anymore. I also know that they were right. Losing weight so fast like I did is bad news, especially going into championship season. I really needed to snap out of it, and I have. Anger might not be the healthiest emotion, but it's better than the self-pity, sadness, and confusion I was drowning in.

"I noticed Gina wasn't there, but thought maybe she had something else going on, or it would have been too much with more than four of you bombarding me."

Lexi turns to me now, looking more serious than I've ever seen her. We've both done our business, washed our hands, and are now lingering by the sinks, trying to keep our conversation in a private space.

"Before you came back, we had a similar conversation with Gina.

Caroline wasn't part of it, just me, Sienna, and Kiki. Hers went a little differently though."

My heart rate picks up. It really sucks being confronted like that, and I can't even imagine how defensive I would have felt if losing weight like I did had been intentional. If I'd been obsessing about my diet. "She didn't take it well, did she?"

Lexi shakes her head. "Gina acted like we were crazy. I mean, I guess I sort of expected some denial, but she was so far from talking about it that the conversation went nowhere."

"Look, are you sure there's something going on?"

Lexi frowns, clearly disliking this question. "Sienna approached *me* about it, without *any* prompting on my part," she replies, and I don't miss the defensive tone in her voice. "You didn't know Gina last year, but she's a lot thinner and a lot faster than she used to be."

"Yeah, but, we run a lot more than I did in high school. I'm sure a lot of bodies change with all this training."

Lexi sighs. "I'd love to be wrong about it, I really would." She sounds defeated, and I pull her in for a hug.

"I'm sorry to question you, and I'm worried about her too. Maybe I just don't want it to be true either."

We break away, and Lexi's cheeks are wet. "You know, you hear about eating disorders at running camps and we had a speaker talk to our high school team once, but it always seemed like something that only happens to other people we don't know. It never seemed real. Sometimes we'd joke about it, even, if we saw a super-skinny runner on another team. But all the things you hear about, I think it's happening to Gina, Pepper, and I don't know how to help her."

Gina's quiet when she joins us later. We're all nosy, grilling her about what happened, but she brushes it off as nothing more than post-race fatigue. When she stands on the top podium, accepting her plaque, I do notice that her body has morphed since the beginning of the season. It's not a healthy runner's physique that stands up there, but a bony frame, with knees and shoulder blades jutting. Her calves and quads are so sharply defined they look like they might break through the skin. Maybe I didn't want to see it before, or it didn't stick out in the midst of so many slight builds that surround me at practice each day. But it's pretty unmistakable now that I'm paying attention, and it's silly that I tried to deny what's going on.

I know Gina has just had the best race of her life, but the smile on her face is a sad one, and I ache for her.

We get back to campus early Sunday morning, and Gran's invited the entire girls' team over to our tiny apartment for brunch. She'd invite the boys' team too, but we simply wouldn't be able to fit everyone inside.

Gran has become the team's grandmother, and she takes her role pretty seriously. When she fractured her hip, it started out with just my roommates joining in visits to see her and do her errands. When my other teammates heard my roommates talking about Gran, they all wanted to meet her, and now my apartment on Shadow Lane has UC runners stopping by daily. Gran's eating it up.

She's outdone herself making brunch, with Lulu's help of course. They must have woken up at the crack of dawn because there's just about every breakfast food imaginable covering our kitchen counter and dining room table.

Gran disappears at some point while we're eating and reemerges from her room with a black trash bag balanced on top of the walker she's been relegated to using for a few months. She's beaming, and there's a twinkle in her eye I rarely see. This exuberance only comes out if she's cheering me on at a race or giving presents.

Proudly, she begins to unload the bag, and my jaw drops when I see she's knit hats for every single person on the team, with our initials included so we don't get them mixed up. They are striped in black and gold, the school colors, with pompoms on the top.

"Is this what happens when you're stuck in bed all day?" I ask when she hands me mine.

Gran grins mischievously. "And you thought I was just in there watching soaps, didn't ya?"

"I could hear the soaps, Gran."

"A girl like me can multitask," she answers proudly. "Made one for Dave, too," she says as she shoves a hat on his head, tugging his little ears through two holes. It's quite possibly the cutest thing I've ever seen, though it only lasts for a second before Dave's tugging it off his head, disgusted.

"Now, if you win Nationals, you'll get matching slippers," Gran announces when we shuffle out later with full bellies and matching hats.

"The slipper socks with moccasin feet?" I ask excitedly. She hasn't made me a pair since last Christmas, and they're getting holes.

"You know the ones," Gran replies.

When we're outside the apartment, Lexi laughs. "Slipper socks with moccasin feet? Dude, those must be the ugliest socks ever!"

I grin. "They're more like a hybrid shoe-sock-slipper combo. And yes, they look really dorky. But sooooo comfortable."

"I'm down to start a new trend," Kiki says. "Think of crocs. They were and still are ridiculous looking, but everyone in this state's got a pair, right?"

"Bunny should patent that shit," Trish remarks, adjusting her hat.

I can't help staring out the window at the Wilders' house as we pass it, wondering what Jace is doing right now. I miss him every day, even though I'm trying to maintain a healthy level of anger. I'm not sure what's going to happen when I run out of it.

CHAPTER SEVENTEEN

I run into Gina on my way out of the bathroom on Monday morning. She's coming in from the hallway, and she's dressed in running clothes, her face flushed. When she sees me, she quickly masks the deer in headlights reaction, though we both know she's been caught.

"Just, do me a favor and don't tattle on me, okay?" Snarky Gina is in full swing.

"Tattle? I'm just wondering why you're doing a double workout today. I thought we had this morning off." I feign a lack of interest, pretending to be only mildly curious.

She hesitates. "I'm not supposed to go to practices for a few days. The medics on Saturday convinced Coach I need a break," she says disdainfully. It makes me wonder what else the medics said, and if she's ignoring all of their advice, or just this bit.

I don't know what to say. I can't claim to know exactly what she's thinking, but I've overtrained before, and I know that sneaking in extra workouts and not listening to your body's signals comes with a strong bout of denial. Nothing I tell her will be news. I'm sure she's heard it all before. She must know that her success at Saturday's meet will be short-lived if she doesn't treat her body right.

"I'm worried about you, Gina. A few days' rest could be really good for you at this point in the season," I say, trying out this approach. I really want to delve into my own story from last cross season, when I listened to my doctor about resting and came back to win Nationals. But I can tell by the way she narrows her eyes and purses her lips that it would fall on deaf ears. She's gearing up to give me one of her snide remarks.

"Well, I wouldn't worry, Pepper. There are plenty of rumors going around that you have your own problems to worry about."

I shouldn't let her egg me on, but I take the bait. "What do you mean?" Maybe, by continuing to talk, we can get into a real conversation about what's going on with her. I can also tell she's trying to get back to her room so our other roommates don't catch her.

Gina rolls her eyes. "Don't you read any running blogs? You passed out in the middle of a race two years ago, you got injured last year, and this year you show up to your first college races skinnier than ever. People think you're anorexic."

She watches the color drain from my face. Gina is being cruel right now, and I wonder if this is the real her, or if she's so deeply lost to her own issues, she's become someone else entirely. That thought briefly brings Jace to mind.

Gina walks to her bedroom and opens the door. "Look, I'm not trying to be mean. I kind of figured you already knew about it. All I'm saying is, people shouldn't judge."

And with that, she closes the door, blocking me out. Googling myself is not something I would normally do, but it's impossible to quash the curiosity, even if I know it will only make me feel awful. I find a conversation thread on a popular running site with the title question: *does Pepper Jones have an eating disorder?*

Okay, so Gina didn't make this up. The thread started a month ago, and there's a photo of me from the California invitational. It might just be the angle, but I do look quite thin. The next post compares photos from Nationals junior year with a photo from my second college invitational. There might be a little difference in the tone of my body, but it's nothing drastic. There are 43 entries, with people speculating that my injury last season might have been a result of anorexia. Of course, it doesn't help that I passed out in the middle of a race junior year.

The entries don't bother me like they might have a year or two ago. People say a lot of things that aren't true on the internet. It sucks, but I've dealt with worse things. Compared to what Madeline Brescoll and Savannah Hawkins did, these posts are nothing. They don't even feel that personal. It bothered me more that my teammates were concerned.

It's not even that weird to see photos of me in the team butt huggers posted by strangers. I mean, the school's website is covered in these photos, and I'm sure they show up in other places on the internet.

No, what I find disturbing is that Gina's read all of these postings. I don't know what that means.

After one week of making a point to eat healthy, regular meals, my skinny jeans are once again snug like they should be. Nothing to worry about here. I spend most of the day wondering if or who I should tell about Gina running this morning. I'm not sure what it would accomplish if I told one of the captains or Coach. I mean, I know she'd be pissed at me. And Coach and the team captains are already clued in that she's not entirely healthy.

In the end, I decide it would backfire. She needs friends and people she can trust right now. She probably already feels like we're all watching her, judging her, as she said. Gina's twenty years old, no longer a child. Being here for her might be all we can do.

The whole situation brings me back to the fall of Jace's senior year at Brockton Public, when he fell too deeply into the drug and partying scene. I can't force people to see their problems or change their ways. I wished I could then with Jace and I wish I could now with Gina. Like I did with Jace, all I can do is be a friend.

As the days go by, and I go from class, to practice, to Gran's, to meals with the team, the fury fades into bitterness and a deep sadness. Jace is a constant in my head and on my heart, and his presence fills me with both resentment and longing.

I miss his smirk. I miss the way he nuzzles my hair when he hugs me. I miss his laugh when he lets down his guard. I miss how his green eyes flash and darken when he's angry or turned on. I miss the calluses on his hands and fingers. I miss the way I felt completely loved and protected in his presence. I don't think I'll ever feel that way again. At least not from him.

I get to run alone on Thanksgiving morning, and I'm grateful for that time on the trail with Dave. I need to prepare myself for several hours in the same room with Jace. We haven't spoken since I came by his apartment and found Melanie there, looking far too cozy. Aside from that brief and not-so-pleasant encounter, it's been longer than we've ever gone without spending time together. I've been simultaneously dreading and craving this day.

Jim and Jace come over for Thanksgiving every year. I could have asked Gran to make other plans, but that felt weak. I already told Jace he was a coward, and I won't be accused of hypocrisy. The good news is that Wallace will be joining us. He's officially Gran's boyfriend, and I'm cool with it. I've met him on a few occasions since her fall in the bathroom, and he seems harmless. He's smitten with Bernadette Jones and I don't blame him.

I choose my outfit carefully. Though it's tempting to wear a pair of jeans I know Jace loves on me, I don't want to be too obvious. Instead, I go with black jeans and a purple sweater that clings nicely to my hips and chest. I'd normally wear something with more give in the waist, but it's unlikely I'll reach the same level of comatose fullness that typically accompanies Thanksgiving Day.

With the walker close by, Gran's in her element in the kitchen. Despite the effort I put into looking nice, I've got on my new pair of slipper socks that Gran gave me this morning. They're school colors.

"Don't tell the rest of your team that you've got those, young lady. I told them you had to win Nationals to get a pair, but you know I don't care about that. I only have a few more pairs to go before I've got them all done."

"Jeez, Gran, do you ever sleep?"

"Ah, the whole knitting club has been at it, but I like to take all the credit," she admits with a wink.

I'm grinning when there's a light knock on the door before the Wilder men let themselves in. My smile falters as I wipe my hands on my apron and look up. Jace avoids looking at me as he wraps Gran in a hug. He doesn't turn to offer me the same greeting, but Jim avoids a potentially very awkward moment by hugging me, and then Gran gets them drinks and goes back to busying herself around the kitchen. I finish my own task and happily engage in talks with Jim about the cross season.

Wallace arrives a few minutes later, wearing cowboy boots, worn jeans, and suspenders with a button-down plaid shirt. He's still got a full head of white hair, which is parted at the side and neatly brushed. The preppy-western-rugged style may or may not be intentional, but it totally works for Wallace. Sometimes when people say someone's "just got their own style" what they really mean is, "the dude has no sense of style." Gran and Wallace though, they each have a true style all their own.

Jim and Jace shake Wallace's hand as they exchange introductions, and I'm surprised to hear Jace say, "I've heard a lot about you from Bunny." Gran mentioned at one point that Jace was calling regularly to check in, and I wonder if that's continued. I'd hate for him to cut out Gran from his life because of me.

It's hard not to look at Jace. It's like fighting a magnetic pull. My eyes are simply drawn to him, and though I try not to stare, I'm processing every detail about him. Having not seen him up close for weeks, the sheer beauty that is Jace Wilder strikes hard. I never have gotten used to it, but when I saw him every day, touched him every day, it didn't shake me like it is right now. Despite that, I don't miss the fatigue etched in his handsome features. The sharp lines that sculpt his chin and cheekbones seem more prominent than usual, and there are dark circles under his eyes.

Though I know I should, I find little pleasure in these signs of Jace's distress. The part of me that was his friend for so many years, that never knew I could have more, simply wants to comfort him and tell him it will all be okay. The pain from losing Annie will lessen with time. It makes me incredibly sad that I almost wish we could go back to that time before we became a couple, when we both squashed any desire for more because we believed it just couldn't, or shouldn't, be.

Gran corrals us all to the dining room table, and I smile as I watch her hold Wallace's arm. "Wally dear, you'll sit here, next to me. You might be the oldest fella here, but me and Jim won't be giving up our spots at the head of the table any time soon."

"Perfectly happy sitting between the Jones girls," Wallace replies. "I don't want to get in the middle of two decades of tradition." It hasn't been quite that long, but still, despite everything that's happened between me and Jace, it feels right when we all settle into our familiar seats.

It's not surprising to discover that Wallace is a fan of Jace Wilder, UC quarterback. Talking football is safe and the conversation flows easily as we shovel heaps of delicious food onto our plates.

"Lotsa talk, boy," Wallace says. "They're sayin' UC might make the Bowl Championship this year."

Jace's eyes brighten a bit for the first time all night. "We've got a shot, Wallace. But it's just talk for now. The team's really focusing on the Conference Championship this year."

Wallace shakes his head in amazement. "Can you believe the team was one of the worst in the conference two years ago?" Wallace gestures to Jace. "Then this boy comes along and now they're shooting for a win. It's somethin' else."

My heart swells with pride. The college bowl is like Nationals for football. It's for the best of every conference. Jace had mentioned over the summer that it was a possibility for the team to go this year. As the season's progressed, everyone's saying that it's looking more and more likely UC will be selected. Of course, it's not only Jace who's turned the team around. His class year was full of top recruits, including his roommate, Frankie Zimmer, who's one of the best college defensive linemen in the nation. Still, they couldn't have done it without Jace.

My stomach churns with emotion. Jace is doing well on the field. I knew this already. I've followed the team's season. As his childhood friend, I'm relieved he hasn't ruined his scholarship or his potential for a football career over his emotional turmoil with his mother. But as his ex-girlfriend, well, that tells me he's still in control. He's got a handle on his life, and he knows what he wants and what he doesn't. A new wave of rejection pummels me as I reach this understanding. I swallow hard to fight the well of emotion that threatens to spill out all over the dining room table.

Would Jace have dumped me whether or not Annie left? As much as I want to believe the answer is no, Jace's calm and detached manner as he chats football and eats his green beans suggest he is utterly unaffected by my presence. The calm, cool and collected Jace Wilder from high school has returned.

And then I remember that Jace hates green beans. It gives him away. He's not even thinking about what he's putting on his plate, or tasting what he's eating. I try to hide my smile, but the thrill at what this means, that his demeanor is a façade, is impossible to hide.

CHAPTER EIGHTEEN

Jace

I've walked up and down the hallway of Pepper's dorm suite too many times to count. I made her a fucking friendship bracelet. What was I thinking? It's sitting in an envelope taped to her door, and I really want her to have it. Even more, I want her to wear it. It's extra long so it will wrap around her wrist a couple times and hopefully never come off, but fuck I feel like such a weirdo doing this. She's moving on, and it's killing me. I want her to move on more than anything, to forget about me entirely. To give up on us. To stop threatening to crack me open every time I see her looking at me like she does. But now that I see her actually getting over me, all I want is to bring her back to me. I'm such an asshole.

I've taped the damn envelope with the bracelet on her door, left, started down the stairs, and returned to take it down three times now. But I keep taping it back up again, wanting Pepper to have a piece of me on her at all times. Not wanting to let her go but knowing I have to. This time, after I've taped it back up and turned to attempt leaving, I run into her roommate Gina Waters coming up the staircase.

She offers a tight, unwelcoming smile before averting her eyes from me. Damn, the girl definitely needs to eat a slice of pizza. She is skin and bone, and looks sick. When she passes me I do a double-take and watch her from behind until she reaches the door, and, ignoring the envelope, goes inside. I never really knew Gina but from what I've observed, she's a pretty weird girl. Kind of standoffish or something. But I definitely do not remember her being this skinny. The girl's got problems, and I hate that her issues are undoubtedly stressing Pepper out. I wish Pepper could talk to me about it, wish I could support her somehow. But I can't. I don't have the capacity to do it, no matter how much I want it. The bracelet will have to do.

PEPPER

The day before we fly to Indiana for Nationals, I find an envelope with my name on it taped to the main door of our dorm suite. Inside, there's a friendship bracelet. It's rough and looks like it was made by a child, but I know better. My box with string and beads is in my dorm room, so unless Jace broke in to borrow it, he must have gone to the craft store himself to get the black and gold colors.

The one he made me my junior year of high school finally fell off this summer, after I'd worn it for a year and a half. I made one with the UC colors for Jace when he went to college last year, and as far as I know, he still has it. This one is long enough to wrap around my wrist twice, and I don't hesitate asking Lexi to tie the knot tight, knowing it won't come off for a long time, and only when it's good and ready, worn through all the way.

There's nothing else in the envelope, just the bracelet, but he doesn't need words to communicate his message. Friendship bracelets might be silly and childish, but the reminder of our childhood, of how many times I made these for Jace, Wes, and Gran, it fills me with a peace I haven't felt in months. It's like warm water, gentle and soothing, cleansing and renewing.

Yet the peace doesn't last, because this symbol around my wrist – which I can't stop playing with when I go to sleep, on the flight, or when I line up behind Kiki and Sienna at the start of the race – it feels like it's also a return to our past. A truce of sorts. It feels like maybe he's telling me we can be friends again, but only if we go back to two years ago, before we took a different path. And I don't think we can do that.

Still, when the gun goes off and the crowds of runners stampede around me, the feel of the soft fabric on my skin grounds me. It makes me feel strong, like I can do anything. The way Jace used to make me feel, and I guess still does, despite his rejection.

Gran couldn't fly out to watch with her hip, so I don't have any family cheering me on this time. I know it's just a stupid bracelet, but it connects me to my family in Brockton, to my past, and to everything that's gotten me to where I am in this moment.

Nationals in college is nothing like high school Nationals. Unlike in high school, where everyone qualifies individually, almost everyone at college Nationals qualifies as part of a team. I like that. It takes the pressure off me personally. There are also about four times as many runners, and the course is wide enough to accommodate everyone.

Somehow, my teammates have managed to stick together in the swarms of runners. All seven of us are very close at each practice and race, but it's still fairly remarkable when we remain in a cluster with only one kilometer to go. I keep looking from side to side, shocked to see the same familiar faces I train with each day beside me. The crowds of people along the sidelines of the course roar with enthusiasm at our solidarity, amazed that even as we gain momentum going up the final hill, no one pulls ahead or drops back. As a team, we pick off other runners until we reach the top, and then the large finish banner is ahead of us.

When Sienna drops the hammer, sprinting with no restraint, I open up my stride with her, knowing that my teammates are all doing the same. It's not easy to reach that next level of pain, and I know I'm not the only one wanting to just give in, back off, and get some reprieve. It reminds me of the hill sprints we did when half the team was hungover. If one of us had given up that afternoon, none of us could have done it. We were in it together then, and we are again now. I just hope I'm not the one to puke this time.

We spread out a little as we each cross the finish, our sprinting abilities not equally matched, but the commentator and the crowds have an emotional response to watching teammates finish one after the other like this in a huge competition with over two hundred runners.

As soon as we've caught our breath, we're a mess of sweaty arms hugging each other. Lexi finds the energy to jump on me and my shaky legs can't hold me up. We tumble to the ground and before I know it, all seven of us are heaped in a pile. It's mostly giggles, but I notice a few tears from our captains. Racing together like we did wasn't planned or expected, which makes it even more special.

I've never witnessed Coach Harding lose his cool, but he's a blubbering disaster when we find him by the team's tent. The boys are warming up for their race, and he's trying to collect himself.

"I'm never going to forget watching the seven of you pace together the entire race. And I think some of the guys on the team might have lost it when you were sprinting to finish in a group like that."

It's not something I'll ever forget either. Our goal at the beginning of this season was simply to qualify as a team for this meet. As the season progressed, it became clear that qualifying wouldn't be much of a challenge, and Coach thought we might even be able to shoot for a podium finish. We didn't have any standout top finishers today, but it's nearly unheard of for everyone on a team to place in the top forty like we did.

After cheering on the boys, we wait anxiously for the award ceremony. With so many competitors, it's hard to get a feel for what place we got overall. Hundreds of runners, fans and coaches sit on a wide hill overlooking the podium, and the energy shifts when an announcer steps forward carrying a clipboard. He delivers individual awards first, naming off the top twenty-five, who earn All-American honors. Sienna finished first for our team, and just made the cut for All-American, but the rest of us missed the cutoff. That might be a cruel irony for some teams, but most of us cheer loudly, far from disappointed. Gina remains quiet, and I'm sure after winning the Conference championship, she hoped to hear her name listed amongst the All-Americans today.

When the announcer finally gets to the team awards, he begins with fifth place. At first, we glance around at each other nervously when he announces third place and we still haven't heard our team. We were certain after our finish today that we'd be up there in the top five, holding our trophy and grinning. Second place is the University of Oregon, and all of us tense up before he announces first. It couldn't be, could it? But there are no other teams who had as many runners in the top half of the race.

"And this year's Women National Cross Country Champion is the University of Colorado!" he finally declares. We're up on our feet, a new round of hugs and giggles and tears erupting as we make our way down the hill.

When we stand on the wood platform, arms slung around each other's shoulders and cameras flashing, I don't think I've ever felt prouder. Not when I won high school Nationals individually the first time. Or the second. Not when Brockton Public won State. The collective effort that went into this spot on top of the podium, looking out at hundreds of cross country runners and fans, it makes the win so much sweeter.

It's late by the time we get back to campus that night. After racing our hearts out and traveling for several hours, I'd wrongly assumed we'd postpone the celebration to another night. The girls have been talking for weeks about how we're going to have one last awesome party after Nationals and before final exams start. It's been months since anyone on the team has been out, and I know they're all going to be in rare form when that party goes down. I just didn't expect it to happen tonight. But I suppose when you win the National Cross Country Championship, you can muster up the energy to celebrate. The boys didn't win, but they got their podium finish with third place.

I am also unprepared for the welcome party that greets us in the field house parking lot. After flying back from Indiana, I found myself falling asleep on the hour-long bus ride from the airport, and I'm rubbing my eyes, trying to rally the energy to keep up with my teammates' enthusiasm to party tonight, when I see the crowds gathered. It's mostly comprised of our teammates who didn't get to compete at Nationals, but I recognize a few others who compete on the track and field team. And of course, Gran is there, waving her arms and wolf whistling as we descend the stairs.

She hugs each of us before asking our shoe size. When she begins fishing out slipper socks for both the men's and women's team members, I notice the broad-shouldered Wilder frame holding out the giant bag for her. But it's not Jace, it's Jim. And beside him, his other son, Wes.

Grinning, I rush up to Wes and throw myself in his arms.

"Man, I have *missed* you!" I tell him.

When we finally pull away, I give Jim a hug too, but not with nearly as much enthusiasm. "I didn't really miss you Jim, sorry."

He laughs. "No hard feelings here, Pep. You did just see me a couple of weeks ago."

"Wait, why aren't you guys at Jace's game? Wasn't today the Conference championship?" I may not be speaking to him, but I do pay attention to his football schedule.

"It's been over for a couple hours, Pep," Jim tells me. "They won."

"Nice. That's awesome." My voice falls flat. It's a huge accomplishment. The UC football team had no chance at this title before Jace joined the team, and I'm proud of him. But I don't feel I have a right to feel pride, because he's not mine anymore. We won't be celebrating anything together tonight.

"Did you come all the way back to watch the game?" I ask Wes.

"No, we have final exams earlier than you guys and I'm home for winter break. I just happened to get in right before the game."

"We're celebrating tonight, if you want to come hang out," I offer.

"Sure, that'd be cool."

I'm surprised by his response, not expecting he'd actually want to hang with a bunch of cross runners his first night back, instead of his friends from Lincoln Academy or with Jace and the football team. Maybe the football team is still lying low since their season isn't over yet.

With howling winds and freezing temperatures, the gathering in the parking lot is short-lived. Wes offers to drive some of us to the yellow house, where a keg is waiting. I've never been with Wes when he doesn't know anyone, but it takes all of two minutes before most of the girls on my team are lusting after him, and the guys are trying to be his buddy. It's a trait he shares with Jace, and the familiarity of the social dynamic with him in the room is comforting. I've kind of missed having a people-magnet as a sidekick.

We find some stools in the kitchen at the center of traffic and where we can see everyone. We're settling in when Ryan pulls up a stool beside us.

"Hey man, how's Princeton? Are you missing Brockton?" Ryan asks.

"Princeton's fun. Between classes and football I haven't had too much time to get real homesick, but it feels good to be back now that I'm here."

"Have you even been to your house yet?" I wonder, remembering he went straight to the game.

"Nope," Wes says easily with a smile. I hate what I know is underneath that smile. There's probably no one there waiting for him, even if his mom and dad are home, which is unlikely.

"When did you get in?" Ryan asks.

"Earlier today, but I went right to the football field to watch the game."

"Oh, yeah. Their win kind of overshadowed the girls' today, but that's cool for Jace. I heard he won MVP for the conference."

Ryan's eyes dart to mine briefly, like I might have the answer. I shrug, trying to hide my hurt. I should know this information. It's huge.

"Yeah man, his phone was blowing up after the game from reporters," Wes says. "We didn't get to spend much time with him because the team is getting him wasted."

My heart tenses and I glance down at my beer as I feel Ryan's eyes on me. I'm pretty sure everyone knows by now that Jace broke up with me, but given that neither of us are talking about it, no one really knows how or why it ended. I'm not sure I really understand it myself. Sometimes people try to bring him up in conversations with me to see what I'll say, but I know Wes isn't trying to do that. If anything, he's trying to fill me in on what's going on with Jace so I'm not caught off-guard.

Kiki approaches us then, sitting down on Ryan's lap with an ease that says she's done it dozens of times. I know they hooked up at one point, but I didn't know it was still going on. If so, it's been months, and I'm surprised a casual no-strings hookup can last so long. Or maybe it's more serious than that. Either way, Kiki's giving him all the signals and it isn't long before they escape upstairs.

Wes charms my teammates for a while longer before a text message comes through, and he looks at me apologetically. "I'm going to take off to meet up with Jace, Pep, hope you don't mind."

I desperately want to know what Jace is doing, how he's doing, where he is. But I don't ask. I just nod. "Yeah, thanks for hanging with us tonight."

"It's late, but there's still a rager going on at Sig Beta," Wes says. "Or, the old Sig Beta," he amends.

Brax overhears our conversation and before I know it, the entire team is trekking across campus to Sig Beta. My anxiety builds the closer we get to Jace. I guess we'll be celebrating at the same place tonight, after all.

CHAPTER NINETEEN

After the day we've had, the mile-long walk feels like an endurance test. We can hear music blaring from several blocks away, but it seems to take forever before we reach the house. By the time we get there, I'm both hungry and thirsty, and since there's no food around, a beer seems the best solution. I've never actually craved a beer until now, and it goes down easily.

"Damn, girl," Trish says in awe as I finish my first one without coming up for air.

"I didn't know you could chug beer like that," Lexi says, handing me another.

"Me neither," I admit.

It takes the edge off the ball of nerves building inside me. Since we broke up, I haven't seen Jace in a setting like this one. We've only run into each other in safe, predictable places like Chapman Hall or the gym. If his teammates are getting him drunk tonight, like Wes said, I have no idea what to expect.

Well, maybe I know exactly what to expect, and that's what I'm so afraid of. I don't know if I can handle seeing a drunk Jace, with girls hanging around, and having no claim over him.

Wes has already disappeared, as he typically does when he hits a big party like this one. I stay with Trish and Lexi, unwilling to get lost alone in these crowds. I've never been to a party with this many people. Or maybe it just seems like more because everyone is inside. It's too packed to move and I find a wall to stick by in order to avoid getting jostled by passing bodies.

It's one in the morning, but it doesn't look like anyone is going home any time soon. Instead, it's the time of night when it's perfectly acceptable, in college at least, to act outrageously stupid. I keep seeing people wearing nothing but underwear, and it takes a while to realize they are members of the cheerleading squad and football team.

"Dude, why are all these people covered in marker?" Lexi whisper-shouts in my ear.

I shake my head, dumbfounded. Drawings and obscenities are on every inch of skin on the nearly-naked bodies.

Trish takes in our confusion, and leans in so we can hear her explanation. "The football team had a highlighter party thing," she says, as if that explains everything.

"I thought you were supposed to wear white to highlighter parties," Lexi responds.

Trish shrugs. "Must not have had time to get white clothes."

"I think people just like being naked," I observe. Besides, despite the frigid temperatures outside, it's a sauna in here. I've already taken off my sweater and I'm still hot.

"That too," Trish says with a grin. "I'd totally strip down right now if I was drunk enough not to think about it."

Lexi raises her eyebrows. "Well, then. I say we need some shots."

I shake my head, unwilling to find out what wild Pepper might bring out tonight. But Lexi has already taken our hands and is dragging us through the throng of people as if she knows exactly where she's going. Before I know it, she's taking us up the stairs and down a hallway. It's still crowded up here. It seems bodies are packed into every square inch of this house. When she opens the last door in the hallway, I'm surprised to find Clayton standing on the other side.

He's not alone. There are a few others sitting around a coffee table, but we're obviously in someone's bedroom. It's a very large room with a balcony and four-poster bed. I have the distinct impression this was once meant for the Sig Beta president, and that means it's likely that Clayton, captain of the baseball team, lives here now.

He smiles widely when he sees us. Though I'm happy to get away from the crowds for a moment, I really hope Lexi isn't planning on making herself comfortable here.

"Hey Lexi, it's been a while, but I see you took me up on my offer from a ways back." The people on the couch watch us curiously and I have little doubt you don't just show up here without an invitation.

She walks toward him with a confidence I admire. "You did say you had the best liquor selection in the house, and we've been in season until a few hours ago, so I never had a chance to see if you were telling the truth."

Harmless flirting comes naturally to Lexi. She's giving Clayton the attention he wants, but she manages to do it without sending out vibes that she'll be doing anything more than talking and maybe having a drink. If only I had such finesse.

"Well, let me fix something for you. Shots for the National Champs?"

He starts to pull out bottles from a cabinet. Lexi asks, "Do you have tequila?"

"Lexi," I protest.

Clayton shows Lexi two choices of tequila, and it doesn't escape my notice when he blatantly checks me out, probably wondering if the alcohol will get me dancing with him again. I don't want to do something I'll regret, but I also need some liquid courage to face Jace tonight. Because I know I will.

I sort of want to throw caution to the wind and see what happens. It's probably a little stupid and careless, but Trish and Lexi do it all the time, and sometimes I wish I could be more like them. They have a little of Zoe Burton in them, and Pepper Jones needs that in her life.

I watch carefully as Clayton pours the shots. After having my drink spiked last year, I'm vigilant about what goes in my drinks. Even if it's tequila, I at least want to control my night of getting out of control. The others in the room join us, and Clayton lifts a toast to the women's cross team before we throw them back. He's not stingy with his liquor, and he's poured us each another shot before I have a chance to contemplate if I'm prepared to let my wild side out for the night. Too late, I think, as the fire spreads from my belly to my limbs, and then to my head.

"Can I check out the balcony before we leave?" I ask. I don't know why I suddenly want to go outside, but before I know it Clayton is opening the door and the others are yelling at us to shut it because it's freezing.

I didn't exactly want anyone out here with me, and I hope Clayton doesn't think I'm trying to make a move on him or something. We stand holding the rail, looking out at the street and the buildings beyond. We're actually standing pretty far apart, and he's not trying to move closer, so I let down my guard.

"Brockton looks like a real city from up here at night." The bright lights against the dark sky are mesmerizing.

"What do you mean? Brockton *is* a real city."

"Yeah, I guess. But I always think of it as a small town, you know?"

I glance over at him and he's studying me. "I know. It's home." He looks back out at the view. "It'll be weird leaving this place."

"Where are you going?"

He shrugs. "Not sure. Somewhere to play baseball, hopefully."

I remember what I learned last year about the team, that a lot of them did steroids. Jace told me it's pretty common on baseball teams. Maybe it's the tequila, or maybe it's that Clayton helped me out not once, but twice, but I boldly ask, "Do you do steroids, Clayton?"

He laughs. Really hard. Like, full-on, gasping-for-breath laughter. And I don't think it's because he found my boldness amusing, although that might have something to do with it. Finally, he answers, "Not anymore, Pepper. People change."

"Believe me, I know." Jace has changed so much over the past few years, I sometimes feel like I don't even know him anymore. For most of high school, we were best friends and nothing more. Then I started dating Ryan, and Jace went all delinquent on me. Ever since Jace and I got together, I thought he'd begun to let go of that dark place inside of him. Maybe part of it was being with me, and part of it was his mom returning to Brockton, but that progress stopped abruptly months ago when she left.

It's like there are always two roads for him, one dark and the other light. He can switch from one to the other too easily, so maybe they are the same road, just one side is in the shade. I think I might have had too much to drink.

"It's freezing, let's go inside," Clayton says, opening the door again. Did I say all that out loud?

Wes opens the door to Clayton's room at the same time we come in from the balcony. His eyes zero in on us like laser beams, taking in the way Clayton is standing beside me, closing the door behind us. I shrug. No one has a claim on me anymore, and I can talk to boys on balconies if I feel like it.

Wes looks away, and I notice the girl with him. I gasp. Dramatically. The others in the room turn to look at me, and their gazes swing between me, Wes, and Veronica Finch, who will always be known to me as pigtail girl. I vow to never wear pigtails. She is friends with Savannah, possibly even conspired with her to hurt me, and therefore she is an enemy. Tequila helps to clarify good and evil, I think.

I march over to Wes. "Do you know who she is?" I ask, pointing at Veronica. Subtlety is not a goal of mine at the moment.

Wes hesitates for a moment, and I wonder if he actually knows that this was, may still be, Savannah's best friend. "Yeah, Vanessa. We just met."

Ah, no wonder he hesitated.

Veronica begins to clarify that her name is not Vanessa, but I interrupt her. "She's friends with Savannah." I'd elaborate, but there's no need. Wes stiffens and points to the door.

"Yeah, okay, well, see you later," he dismisses her.

She puts her hands on her hips. "Are you kidding me?" She looks ready to say more, but Clayton puts a hand on her shoulder and not-so-gently guides her out of the room.

"You're not wanted here, Finch. And it's *my* room."

I don't even feel sorry for her when she struts out of there like she's hot stuff. She is kind of hot, I guess. I mean, in an evil sort of way. I feel powerful, and totally justified. Girls like that are bad news, and she doesn't deserve a piece of Wesley Jamison.

After Veronica leaves, and with Wes in the room, I decide I much prefer it here to the rest of the party. Lexi and Trish seem happy enough as well, each flirting with a baseball player. Lexi stopped hooking up with Brax at some point, and I'm not entirely sure why. I think they were both too afraid to admit their feelings to each other and they couldn't keep doing what they were doing and pretending it was meaningless. I have a feeling that kind of thing happens a lot in college, and it makes me sort of sad.

At some point, I notice that the number of people in the room is growing. It's still not as crowded as it was downstairs, but while the room is big for a bedroom, it's not exactly large enough to host a party. I've designated myself the room's DJ, and I'm actually enjoying myself as I sort through the music collection and chat with random people. When I spot Melanie the redhead across the room, mixing a drink, I push down the ugly feelings as best I can.

Only a moment after I see her, Jace enters the room. I've heard people say things like, *I felt him before I saw him*, and for the first time, I actually experience that sensation. But unlike when it's a serial killer or something in the room, my body flashes hot instead of cold. My head snaps up against my will, seeking him out.

Sure enough, he's wandering over to Wes, wearing nothing but a pair of boxer briefs, with marker all over his back, chest and arms. I have little doubt his teammates had something to do with his attire. I notice he doesn't appear drunk, and though I haven't seen him drunk in a very long time, for some reason I expected it tonight. If I'm honest, I was actually looking forward to it. I think I was secretly planning to corner him and grill him on what happened to us, with the hope that he'd let his guard down. I don't know why I thought that was a good idea, or that it would be at all fruitful.

Even with Clayton and Wes in the room, there's a shift in energy with Jace's arrival. Sometimes I wonder if I imagine it, but right now it's unmistakable. People turn their bodies toward him, look his way, track his movements. I wish I was immune, but I'm just as affected as everyone else. The boxer brief situation is not helping.

This time, though, I won't wait for him to come to me. I won't be the coward in this relationship. My steps falter at that thought. There is no relationship. But I charge forward anyway.

"Hi, Jace."

"Hi, Pepper. Congrats on the big win today."

"Yeah, you too. And the MVP award. That's awesome."

"Thanks."

"Nice outfit."

Jace glances down and sighs. "Yeah. Couldn't get out of it."

Wes looks back and forth between us, clearly amazed that it's possible for things to be this awkward. Yup. It has come to this. We are acting like acquaintances. Like we have no history at all.

I stay for a few minutes, looking for an opening, any opportunity to go deeper, but the conversation remains surface level. Finally, I can't stand it.

"Why the bracelet, Jace?" I hold up my wrist. "What was it all about?"

I scour his reaction for any sign of what he's feeling, but I come up short.

"Oh, I'm glad you liked it. Did you wear it at the race?"

I nod.

"I guess it was good luck after all, then."

I blink rapidly, trying to comprehend how he can act like this means nothing.

"Yeah, I guess so," I whisper.

It's time for me to go. I can't get out of the room fast enough. I thought he'd come up to Clayton's room for me. To see me and talk to me. But he probably came for Melanie. I feel so stupid. I thought I had accepted that things were over. I thought I had decided not to shed another tear over him.

I guess I can decide whatever I want, but I can't control my emotions like Jace can. Or maybe he's not controlling them. Maybe he just doesn't feel anything toward me anymore.

Before I go to bed that night I take my scissors and cut the bracelet off. I can't bring myself to toss it in the trash, but I place it in a shoebox with some of my running medals, and slide it under my bed. All signs of Jace Wilder must stay hidden from view.

CHAPTER TWENTY

When I return to the dorms after my last exam a week and a half later, I'm experiencing a level of exhaustion almost as severe as the final mile of a cross race, only it's mostly in my head this time. Since the post-Nationals party, I've been doing nothing but study. I guess I eat and sleep and I've gone on a few runs, but for the first time ever, school work has briefly taken over my life.

Indoor track and field officially started weeks ago, and the first meet is this weekend, but all of the cross runners who went to Nationals are supposed to take a few weeks off from workouts and just focus on recovering so that we can come back from winter break rested and ready to start track season. I hadn't been entirely neglecting my school work before finals started, but the final exams and papers in my classes count for over half my grade for the entire semester, and the amount of material involved was daunting, to say the least. But I wasn't alone. The entire campus was on lockdown.

I drop my backpack in my room and head to the restroom, trying to decide whether I want to take a nap or go on a run. I've finished my first semester of college and it seems anticlimactic to go to sleep, even if that's what my body craves. But when I open the door to the bathroom and hear the distinct sound of someone throwing up, I snap to attention. It's two PM and unlikely any of my roommates have been drinking enough to puke. The sound is accompanied by a pungent smell and then the toilet flushes and Gina swings open the stall door.

"Oh, hi Pepper," she says lightly, turning on the faucet to wash her hands. "Did you just get back from an exam?"

"Yeah," I reply cautiously. "Are you ok? Are you sick or something?" I'm quite certain that is not the case, but I have no idea how to handle this.

She shrugs as she wipes her hands with a paper towel. "No, I'm fine."

"But, weren't you just puking?"

"Yeah, sometimes I throw up before a test. Nerves, you know?"

I shift my weight back and forth, unwilling to move from my spot. I'm blocking the door, and Gina is waiting for me to get out of the way. But I can't. I have to say something. Do something. But what?

"Um, do you throw up on purpose?"

Gina straightens her shoulders. "Yeah. I mean, it's better than letting it out in the middle of the test, don't you think?" she asks sharply.

"How often do you do it?"

"I don't know. Look, Pepper, I've really got to get going." She sounds impatient now, like this silly conversation is a waste of her time. Like what just happened is no big deal. I almost feel stupid for pushing it.

"Gina, you're making yourself throw up. That's not something I can ignore."

Her eyes narrow and I know I've hit a nerve. "Not everyone can be skinny without effort, Pepper. Some of us have to work for it. I know it's not a reality you'd understand, but I suggest you stop questioning me. I'm perfectly capable of making my own decisions. Sometimes I want to eat things that will make me fat and throwing up after keeps the weight off. It's life." And with that, she bursts by me, letting the door slam behind her.

Stunned and certainly unable to take a nap now, I find myself jogging to Shadow Lane and sitting at the kitchen counter, telling Gran what just went down. "What am I supposed to do?" I ask.

"She needs help, Pep. You need to tell someone who can help her."

"I know, Gran, but who? I can tell Coach or someone on the team, but no one can force her to see a doctor." It's tempting to just tell Lexi, because she was the one who first came to me about Gina. But the more people I tell, the more likely Gina's life will get rolled around in the gossip mill. Lexi isn't inclined to do that to Gina, but I need a plan before I start telling anyone.

"Your coach probably *can* force her to go see a doctor, you know," Gran tells me. "Doesn't he have a say in who's on the team? Can't he keep people out for injuries or health reasons? I think he's the best person to handle this."

"Should I tell Sienna or Kiki, or Lexi or Caroline? Everyone's been worried about her. I just feel like our teammates care about her and want to be involved in helping her but I also feel so disloyal to Gina telling anyone what I witnessed."

Gran nods. "Why don't you talk to Gina? Tell her your concerns, and that you don't feel you can keep this to yourself."

"Gran, she's in total denial and this wicked mean side of her comes out when I've confronted her before. Like, she gets super defensive. I think she might have split personalities," I add.

"Don't get overdramatic now, Pep. I'm sure her body's eatin' up any sweetness left in her, is all."

"Oh? Is that why everyone gets grumpy when we're hungry? Our body eats up our sweetness?"

"Course! That's why we got plenty of cookies in this house at all times. And why I'm such a sweetie," Gran adds with a wink.

I roll my eyes. "Okay, I'll email Coach and ask to meet with him. And I'll try to talk to Gina again."

Gran nods. "Good girl. Now, when are you coming home for the winter break? Your last exam was today, right?"

"Yup. I'm just going to go back to the dorms now, pack up some stuff, have dinner with some people, and then I'll be back in my own bed tonight. Oh, and Zoe might come over later after she gets in," I add.

Gran claps her hands. "Oh goodie. We really need to get some dance parties going while she's home. Don't want to lose my moves in my old age."

"I'm sure Zoe would love to bust a move or two with you, Gran, but you better take it easy on that hip," I warn. Gran likes to pretend nothing happened, but she's not as agile as she was before she fell, that's for sure.

"I can still work it, Pep, don't you worry 'bout me."

"Never, Bernadette, never." I just can't help myself sometimes.

She narrows and points her finger at me. "Careful, or I'll hide all the cookies I've been baking for your homecoming."

Seeing Zoe again feels so good. We've both made new friends and memories over the past few months, but she's still her loveable, bubbly self. And it doesn't surprise me when she mentions a party she wants to hit up.

"Aren't you exhausted from exams, dude?'"

Zoe laughs. "'Dude?' Really? Did college make you cool or something, Pepper?"

I shove her playfully. "No, I'll never be cool, Zoe. But Lexi says 'dude' in like, every sentence, so it kind of rubbed off on me."

"I need to meet this Lexi."

"You'll like her."

"I like her!" Gran calls from the sofa.

"She's got Bunny's stamp of approval, so she must be a good one."

"She's a keeper."

"So anyway, *dude*," Zoe says, "you should come out with me. Everyone's back for winter break. It'll be fun."

"I know you have endless energy, Zoe, but I'm seriously running on empty here. I need fifteen hours of uninterrupted sleep."

Zoe waves me off. "You can get it later. Just come for a little and you can leave whenever."

Sighing, I relent, like I usually do with her. "Fine, where is it?"

She grins. "It's Wes's party."

I don't want to admit why this motivates me to change out of the sweats I've been wearing for a week straight and into a cute outfit. If it's Wes's party, Jace will be there. I must be masochistic to want to see him again, but I can't help it. I didn't run into him once over finals week, since I wasn't at the gym or Chapman Hall at the same times as him like usual. There's a chance he won't show, as he's probably super busy with football training. But the possibility of him being there has butterflies in my stomach. I try to ignore it, knowing these feelings are stupid. I just can't seem to give up on him.

It's been a long time since I've been to a party at Wes's house, and it's strange being here with everyone from Brockton Public and Lincoln Academy, now that we've all graduated. Our high school identities are still with us, but we each come with a new identity too. The house is almost as packed as it was the other night at Sig Beta, and I realize it's not just people from my year and Wes's year, but there are people who graduated before us and people still in high school too. I'm surprised I didn't hear about this party earlier, but knowing Wes, he probably pulled it off last minute.

I spend most of the night hanging out with my old teammates in a big room in the basement. Jenny and Rollie are still together, and they are cuddled up looking far too adorable as we all catch up on our lives over the past few months. We've stayed in touch a little, but there are plenty of stories to share. I'm thankful no one asks me about Jace, whom I still haven't spotted tonight. I've got my Jace-radar turned all the way up though.

The last person I expect to run into when I head to the restroom is Madeline Brescoll. I haven't seen her in a very long time. She disappeared from the Brockton social scene after unsuccessfully trying to sabotage my relationship with Jace. Seeing her coming out of the bathroom, I'm reminded of a time almost two years ago when she cornered me by a bathroom at another party. I'm a lot stronger now than I was then, but I'm not in the mood to deal with a confrontation.

And, judging by the way she shrinks to the side to let me pass and averts her gaze to the floor, Madeline Brescoll is weaker than she once was. But she's still standing there when I come out a minute later, and this time she looks up at me.

"I came here to see you, Pepper," she says quietly.

I stiffen. "Why?"

"I wanted to apologize to you for what I did. I was jealous and I handled my jealousy all wrong. I'm really sorry for all the mean things I did."

Whoa. Totally didn't see this coming. "Um, thanks?" My mind reels, wondering if she has an ulterior motive. I'm sure she's heard about Jace breaking up with me, so that can't still be her goal.

"I also wanted to apologize to Jace. Do you know if he's here?" she asks.

Now I'm even more suspicious. I don't think I'll ever trust this girl. "I don't know." Before she can say more, I turn and leave, not caring all that much about her evil plots. I don't think there's much she can do to hurt me at this point, at least not when it comes to Jace. I don't have him so I have nothing to lose.

Turns out I was wrong. So very wrong.

I decide to head up to the kitchen to grab some drinks for my friends. After running into a few acquaintances from Brockton Public, I see a familiar set of shoulders leaving the kitchen. I'd recognize Jace's back anywhere, but I'm intrigued by the new haircut. He's had a faux-hawk for years and it almost seems like he started the trend himself. Even before he cut it that way, his hair was always a little long and disheveled. Tonight, Jace Wilder is sporting a buzz cut for the first time ever.

Without thinking, I follow him. I want to get a better look. By the time I get out of the kitchen, he's at the far end of the hallway by the study, away from the crowds and leaning against the wall, listening to someone talk whom I can't see. His arms are crossed and he's got a standoffish vibe going on. Or maybe it's the haircut that gives him attitude. The angles and edges of his face are more pronounced, and I have the strange urge to take a picture of his profile. I wish I was closer so I could see his eyes. I bet they pop even more than usual.

My wish is granted when he lifts his head and turns my way. Our eyes lock and I suck in a breath at the intense desire to get closer to him. My suspicion is true. Without the distraction of his unruly hair, his green eyes are mesmerizing.

When he looks away, I still can't move from my spot in the entry way. People are coming and going from the front door, and I'm probably in their way, but I can't tear my eyes away when I see it's Madeline he's talking to. She said she was going to apologize, but as the crowds blocking my view move away, and I'm able to see their entire bodies, Jace puts his hand around her waist, and pulls her body flush against his.

I want to run away. I want to scream at him. Hit him. But I can't do anything except stare. My jaw drops and my eyes blink rapidly, like maybe it will all go away and I'll wake up any second now.

But then his mouth descends to hers and a moment later he takes her hand and pulls her into the study. I don't know how much longer I stand there before Zoe finds me.

"Jace just…" I stutter, unable to say it. "He went in there with Madeline."

Zoe looks in the direction I'm pointing. "What?"

"He kissed her." I can hear the disbelief in my voice as I say it.

"What the hell is wrong with him?" Zoe growls. "After what she did?"

"He saw me. He wanted to hurt me." And he did hurt me. But not because I'm jealous. I know he didn't want her. I don't know what they're doing in that room right now, but it doesn't matter. Jace intended to be cruel. He wants me to hate him. And he accomplished it. The pain is worse than when he shut me out, when he told me things were over, or when I found Melanie in his room. Because I truly feel like the very worst of him has taken over, and I no longer believe he'll come back around one day. He is lost.

As Zoe pulls me away and takes me back downstairs, my feelings for Jace Wilder are no longer muddled and confused. It's not a mix of longing, sadness, regret, pity, and anger because I don't think I'll ever forgive him. Those butterflies? Dead. Hope we could recover from this breakup somehow? Gone. I never thought I'd lose respect for my childhood best friend, neighbor, and first lover. Tonight, there's no more admiration for the boy I wanted for so many years. I think I might even hate him.

JACE

Pepper's in the kitchen rummaging through the fridge when I get to Wes's place. She's bent over, and my body betrays me when it starts to move in her direction, wanting to grab her hips and pull her close. It wants her so bad. The urgency to go to her, to just let down all my walls and melt in her arms, begging for forgiveness and her love, is so overwhelming that I almost can't stop myself. It takes all my willpower to back up, turn around, and leave the kitchen.

I've been acting like a total stalker, keeping tabs on her from afar, making sure she's doing okay. All the guys on my team know to watch out for her and they let me know if she's out at parties, or how she's doing. They don't question it. Pepper's my girl, even if she doesn't know she is anymore.

But she doesn't need me or my teammates watching out for her anymore. Hell, I'm probably the biggest reason for any harm to come her way. Pepper has friends who love her and will keep an eye out for her. She's rocked the transition to college, even without me beside her. The realization is brutal. It really makes me hurt in ways I don't even want to admit. But this is what I wanted. It's why I hurt her.

The pull she still has on me, though, sends a spark of anger and resentment through me that I've only ever directed at myself and my mother. But this time, I feel it toward Pepper. She has the power to break me. My mother couldn't even do that. My mother just made me never want to feel, but I still function. Pretty fucking well, if you ask NFL scouts.

Madeline Brescoll tugs my arm, demanding my attention, and I don't even care enough to shut her down. She starts spewing apology bullshit, but I sense Pepper nearby and my emotions are starting to crumble. I glance up and see her, and the hope in her eyes makes me lose myself. Pepper never hides anything. And I see it. She still loves me. Still wants me. That isn't right. She doesn't need me. She shouldn't want me. Just seeing her looking at me like this is pure agony, and it makes me lose it. I almost hate her for loving me so much.

So I do what I know will change that. Maybe now Pepper won't have control over me anymore.

Kissing Madeline feels wrong on so many levels, and as soon as we're in the study and out of Pepper's line of sight, I push her off me. I'm not sure I'll ever be able to kiss anyone else after Pepper. Yeah, Pepper will always have a hold on me. I'm an idiot to think otherwise.

CHAPTER TWENTY-ONE

Hating Jace is strangely liberating. He's nothing to me now but a weak and hateful ex-boyfriend, and that truth simplifies my life. I don't sit around during winter break wondering when I'll see him or what he's doing. Instead, I hang out with all my favorite Brockton people, throw numerous impromptu dance parties with Gran in our apartment, and try not to bury my emotions with numbness or outrageous runs like I have in the past. There might be a shot or two of tequila involved in this anger coping, and plenty of cookies to keep my sweetness alive, but I'm determined to go back next semester a new woman. Totally single and independent from Jace Wilder.

So, when Wes invites all of us to his parents' ski house the last weekend of winter break, I decide to go whether or not Jace will be there. His presence or absence will not affect my decision. I don't ski, but I'll find something to do. Zoe and Wes have rekindled their relationship – or whatever it is – for winter break, at least. Along with Wes's Lincoln Academy friends, and a few Brockton Public people, Lexi is coming too. She's just come back to the dorms to train for indoor track, and she seems to think snowboarding can't be much different from surfing. Coach will not be pleased if she breaks her legs, so I'm hoping she doesn't do anything stupid.

I know the football team has their final game of the season next Saturday. The local news station Gran likes won't shut up about it. So, even though I'm not concerned with Jace's whereabouts and I hate him, I'm a little surprised to find he's already at the house with Wes when we arrive Saturday morning. Absolutely no butterflies flutter.

We convince Lexi that learning to snowboard in one day is both unlikely and unwise, and she agrees to snowshoe with us instead. Ryan has skied before but says he's terrible and it isn't worth risking being out for the track season. I think his logic is what helps persuade Lexi. While others head out to ski or snowboard, the four of us set out on a mission to summit a nearby mountain on a trail recommended by the snowshoe rental shop. I don't know what Jace does and I don't care.

Over the past few months, Ryan has become someone I can call a friend again. We aren't as close as we once were, but there's none of the awkwardness we struggled with before. He's not much different to me than Zeb, Brax, or some of the other guys on the team.

The hike takes us nearly eight hours because we get lost on the way back, and by the time we return to the house, I'm starving. Someone's ordered pizza. A lot of pizza. Zoe and Ryan head off to shower but Lexi and I can't turn away from the pizzas. As I stuff my face, I think of Gina, and wonder how she's doing.

"Hey, did you talk to Gina at all over break?" I ask Lexi.

Lexi takes her time responding, slowly chewing a mouthful of pizza. "Yeah, I did," she says solemnly. "She's not coming back this semester."

I drop the pizza in my hands, feeling suddenly sick. I went to Coach's office the day after I found her puking in the bathroom and told him that she needed to see a doctor and get help. He reassured me I'd done the right thing, but he didn't say what he was going to do. I tried to get in touch with Gina to talk to her before she went home for break, but I couldn't track her down and she hasn't answered my calls.

"Why isn't she coming back?"

"She called me the day after Christmas, hysterical. She said her parents are making her go to a facility for people with eating disorders."

"For the entire semester?"

"I'm not sure. I guess it depends on how she does. It might only be a few weeks. Honestly, it was a little hard to figure out what was going on. From the sound of it, her parents took one look at her and dragged her to a doctor."

"And whatever the doctor had to say was not good, I take it?"

"Nope."

So it was her parents. Not Coach. I wonder if he had anything to do with it. I wonder if he spoke with her parents. I decide to tell Lexi about what I saw. I can't keep it to myself any longer. I don't want to be the only one on the team who knows how serious it was, and it sort of feels like I'm hiding something. Lexi does not seem surprised by what I share with her.

"I kind of figured she was doing that. I mean, I'd watched her binge eat and then go to the bathroom more than once. With her weight loss and eating habits, it was a logical conclusion."

"At least she's getting help, right?"

Lexi shakes her head. "Dude, I really hope wherever they sent her is a good place. She acted like her parents were crazy, like there's nothing wrong. It's messed up."

We finish eating our pizza in silence before Ryan passes through, heading to the hot tub and suggesting we join. By the time we change into our bathing suits, the hot tub is already filled with people. It's the biggest one I've ever seen, almost pool-size, and we're able to squeeze in beside Wes and Zoe.

As everyone chats about the ski day, I ignore Jace's presence on the other side of the tub.

"So, did your twelve-mile hike today count for your workout or are you crazies going back out for a run tonight?" Wes teases, looking at me, Lexi, and Ryan.

"It's our last weekend of rest before track season starts, Wes, so we get to take a day off," I tell him.

"Wait, a twelve-mile hike in the snow is a day off?" Remy Laroche, a friend of ours from Brockton Public, asks.

"Any day not running is a day off. Don't you know runners are the ultimate badasses?" Lexi asks proudly. "I thought you were friends with Ryan and Pepper in high school. You should know this."

"Well then, you guys should join us on the slopes tomorrow if you're such badasses," Remy challenges.

"I'm down," Lexi quickly agrees.

I shake my head adamantly. "No way."

"Good call, Pepper," Ryan agrees. "My dad would probably give me shit for letting you ski for the first time the day before your first college track practice."

"Oh, come on, man," Wes eggs on Ryan. "I'll take her with me on the easy slopes."

Ryan laughs. "You can still crash into a tree on easy slopes, Wes."

"Nah, I could put her on one of those bungee leash things for little kids," Wes jokes. "You should totally do it, Pep. I'll watch out for you."

"It's really not your job to watch out for Pepper, Wes," Jace's deep voice comes unexpectedly from the other side of the hot tub.

The jovial atmosphere goes cold. Wes shifts forward in his seat and his arm around Zoe slips away. "What are you trying to say, Jace?" he asks. It's a challenge, and I have the distinct impression there's something deeper underlying this exchange.

"You know what I'm saying," Jace says, the hardness in his voice unmistakable.

"No, I think you should spell it out," Wes answers with narrowed eyes.

Jace smirks and I know the words about to come from his lips are ones I do not want to hear. But I can't move. I'm holding my breath, certain that this isn't a new argument brewing. Why Jace is pouncing on Wes tonight, at this moment, is anyone's guess. But this tension between them is an old one, and it's been building for a long time. I can feel it with the way the little hairs on my arms rise, despite the hot water on my skin.

"You want me to spell it out? Fine. You've been in love with Pepper for ages. You've wanted her ever since we were kids. It's about time you let it go. You never got over her and it's been years." His words are delivered with cold authority. But then he lets out a dark chuckle. "Hell, that's probably why you stayed last year, isn't it?"

Wes doesn't answer right away, and I can't look at him. I wonder if he's as shocked as I am.

Jace continues, "It is, isn't it? You didn't want to be thousands of miles away from her, even when she was with me."

Wes cuts Jace off before he can say anymore. "That's why *you* stayed, *brother*." I suck in a breath at his use of that word, hoping the others don't register its significance. The siblings seem oblivious to everyone but each other. "Don't put your shit on me," Wes continues. "You're the one with the issues, not me. I think you might be doing some projecting of your own feelings."

I can't take this anymore. Listening to them hurt each other and letting them use me to do it is wrong on so many levels.

"Stop!" I shout, and the sound echoes. "Just, stop," I say quietly, suddenly exhausted. The weight of Jace's and Wes's gazes on me is heavier than all the dozen others' in the hot tub combined when I hurriedly hop out, snag a towel, and rush inside.

I've been so much better at reeling it in and sorting through my feelings without going for a run, but I don't even try to talk myself out of it as I pull on winter running clothes and lace up. I've got to get away from this house and everyone in it. I've got to feel my legs pounding beneath me.

It's dark out with no street lighting, forcing me to jog at a snail's pace. I don't want to analyze the conversation that just went down. The thing is, if I look back on every memory with Wes over the years, I'm afraid what I might find. But I'm not sure it even matters if there's truth to either of their statements. It doesn't change anything.

I jog down the hill toward the ski village, where there's more light from restaurants, shops and bars. It's Saturday night in the middle of winter, the busiest time of year in this ski village, and plenty of people are still out. The roads through the village are narrow and pedestrian-only, shoveled free of ice and snow. I get a few odd looks, but they don't bother me.

The pizza from earlier sits heavy in my stomach and my legs are sluggish from the hike and hot tub. I've jogged through the entire village and it's too dark on the roads leading off to houses to venture far. It hasn't been long, but it's time for me to go back and face the music.

The first person I see when I try to sneak in through a side door is Zoe. She's got her bag slung over her shoulder, and she looks upset.

Shit. I didn't even think of how that conversation would affect her. I'm so selfish.

"You all right?" I ask hesitantly.

"Shouldn't I be asking you that?"

I nod at her bag. "Where are you going?"

"I thought I'd crash in the bunk room with you and Lexi. It's just too awkward staying with Wes tonight after that," she admits. Zoe is the ultimate optimist, able to brush off just about anything. I though she and Wes were only messing around over break because it was familiar and easy. I never thought they had serious feelings for each other.

But Zoe's eyes are red, and I know she's hurt.

"Dude, I really don't think it's true. Jace was just being an asshole. He's trying to destroy all his relationships by hurting anyone who loves him." It's so messed up and so straightforward at the same time. Maybe it's that simple, but maybe not. I'm done trying to figure him out.

Zoe shrugs. "Yeah, but still, Wes goes back to Princeton in a couple days anyway. It's no big deal."

I take her bag and lead her back to the bunk room before hopping in the shower. After taking my time changing into comfy clothes, I venture through the house, wondering who, or what, I'll find.

It seems everyone has congregated in the rec room. There are about fifteen of us, and enough games in the room to distract everyone from the hot tub showdown. I carefully avoid Wes at the foosball table and Jace playing shuffleboard, deciding to join Remy, Lexi, and Zoe at the card table.

They're playing Euchre, a game that requires two teams of two people. Zoe just lost her partner to a ping pong match, so I'm in luck. With four competitive people involved, the card game provides the perfect distraction. The harsh look on Wes's and Jace's faces when they exchanged those words lingers in the back of my mind, but everyone seems intent on pretending it never happened and I am totally on board with that approach.

When couples start to shuffle off to bed and Remy ditches the game to smoke a joint, I make the decision that a girls-only dance party is absolutely necessary. An old boom box and CDs have been staring at me from a shelf while I played cards, and I know that getting her groove on will help Zoe recover from her funk.

I find a few decent CDs for my purposes, put the boom box under my arm, and announce my intentions, emphasizing the "girls-only" instruction. If no one follows, I am totally cool with getting down by myself. Zoe and Lexi are at my side as we find an unoccupied guest room. It's huge and there are no signs anyone's crashing here, so I get the 90s club hits going and find my place in the middle of the king-size bed.

With the door shut tight, the three of us work up a serious sweat as we go through one CD after the next. It's three in the morning and I've almost lost my voice from all the screaming/singing I've been doing when the door to the bedroom opens.

It's Jace.

I stop dancing immediately and Lexi and Zoe follow suit.

"Shit, it's freezing in here. Why are all the windows open?"

"We got hot dancing. And it's girls only. Get out."

"This is my room."

"Too bad. I don't see any bags in here or your name on the door," I reply.

"Yeah, too bad, jerkface," a slightly drunk Zoe answers. Actually, I don't think she's had anything to drink. She has no barriers totally sober. It's awesome. "This isn't your house and it's not your room."

Jace crosses his arms, not one to back down. "This is where I always stay when I come up here. And all the other beds are taken."

I frown. I'd only been up here a few times as a kid and this is the first time Wes has invited me recently. Whatever.

"Guess you can have the top bunk in the kiddie room with Ryan," Lexi offers. And then she jumps down from the bed, and begins pushing him out the door. Well, she tries pushing him. He doesn't budge. And suddenly I have the urge to embrace my juvenile side. Okay, maybe I've been acting juvenile all night. I'm not afraid to admit it.

I jump down from the bed, screaming, "No boys allowed!"

Zoe's right behind me, pumping her fist in the air. "Yeah, no jerk-faces allowed!"

And the three of us successfully push him out into the hallway, slamming the door and locking it behind us and then erupting into giggles.

When we finally pile into the huge bed together, I grin at our ridiculous behavior. We managed to turn a potentially very bad night around. I hear Zoe humming "Girls just wanna have fun," beside me, and I hug her before falling asleep.

CHAPTER TWENTY-TWO

Three Months Later

I don't think I'll ever love track as much as cross country, but there is something to be said for having clear-cut goals and results. The track doesn't lie. A mile on the UC home track is the same as a mile on any other track. It makes it a little boring, maybe, but there's comfort in it too.

I've been better about figuring out who I am as a runner, as a college runner, and what I've discovered is that my place at a meet or my time on the track does not define my worth as a person, friend, or teammate. That doesn't mean I don't enjoy chasing after a goal, and today I not only hit mine in my very first ten-kilometer race, I smashed it. An indoor track is shorter than an outdoor track, and the longest distance for the indoor track season is a 5K race, which isn't especially exciting, since it's about the same distance as a cross race, only without the fun parts like puddles, mud and hills.

I knew exactly what pace I had to run each lap in order to get the qualifying time for outdoor track and field nationals. We just finished our indoor season, and instead of resting, Coach thought a few of us should go straight to another meet to try to get the qualifying times before resting and beginning another training cycle. After all, it's one of our only home track meets, and it's worth it for convenience alone.

At lap twenty of twenty-five, I was still exactly on pace, along with Caroline, Sienna, and a few girls from other schools. They are the only other ones who will race the longest track distance with me this season. With five laps to go, my body was stressed, but I was actually feeling a little bored. I'd been staring at the back of Sienna's head for a while without much change of scenery from lap to lap, and it was time to spice things up.

I wasn't the only one blown away with what my body had in store for the last mile. My time is now the leading 10K time in the nation on the outdoor track, which sounds fancy but actually isn't saying all that much, since very few have actually competed in a meet so far this season. Still, I'd say my debut in the 10K was a success. The longer the race, the better I seem to do, and I wonder if I'll run a marathon someday.

Caroline, Lexi and I are getting ready for a barbeque at the yellow house after the race. Lexi races the mile in track, and all three of us hit the qualifying standard today, so we're feeling pretty proud of ourselves. Unfortunately, getting the qualifying time doesn't necessarily mean you get to go to Nationals. There are a set number of people in each event, and if more than that amount hit the qualifying time, not everyone gets to go. My time today will probably get me in, but Caroline and Lexi won't know until the end of the season.

Gina's empty room is a constant reminder of what she's going through, and I don't think any of us have gotten used to her being gone. Even though she wasn't herself, she was still part of our dorm foursome and a member of the team, and her absence is like a missing link. Despite our attempts to contact her, she hasn't been in touch with any of us. It sucks.

There are two others I haven't been in touch with since winter break. Wes came by the apartment before returning to Princeton and apologized for the "stuff going on" between him and Jace. He didn't elaborate and I didn't probe.

I see Jace around campus occasionally, but I've given up even trying to pretend we're acquaintances. He acts like he doesn't know me and in return I try to pretend he's a stranger. And that he's ugly. Which he is, on the inside. I think.

The UC football team won the National bowl in January. When I found out, I had a revelation of sorts. Jace chose football. He didn't let that go. The risk of losing the sport he's so passionate about didn't scare him away like I did. He once told me he needs me more than he needs football, or anything else. He was wrong. Or he lied. Either way, I guess I'm happy for him. Happy he didn't throw it all away, let partying, drugs, or girls drag him down. He remained committed to something, and that gives me hope that he'll be all right.

It also made me realize that I can make as many excuses as I want for Jace, but in the end, he broke up with me not just as his girlfriend, but as his friend too. I need to move on just like he has. And I'm doing it. It's not easy. Every day I miss him, but it's getting a little better.

Lexi and Zoe think I need a rebound guy, but that's not me. The first time someone hit on me a few weeks ago – at least, I think they were hitting on me – I panicked. I really don't go out much like some of my teammates do, because I'm convinced the main purpose for most of them is to flirt and hook up with someone. I'm trying to figure out how to be social in this college world as a single girl who doesn't want a hookup, or a boyfriend. It seems I'm a rarity.

It's one of the first warm days of spring, and a bunch of track and field teammates are in the backyard at the yellow house while Zeb mans the grill. I think Caroline has a crush on him, because I always catch her watching him. She's not as shy as I originally thought, she just likes to evaluate the situation before diving in. Zeb, for example, comes off a little cocky and might be a bit of a player, but he's super loyal and I have a feeling when he falls in love with the right girl, it'll be all over him. Caroline has seen this about him and for her sake, I hope Caroline's that girl.

Finding an unoccupied lounge chair, I settle in with my soda, content to relax and observe my friends. Kiki and Sienna try to get me to join in playing Frisbee, but I'm in the mood to be lazy. I'm comfortable enough with my friends now that I feel no obligation to be especially social and I'm still staked out in my chair when I notice the numbers in the backyard have grown considerably.

"Want a burger, Pep?" Zeb calls from the grill, spatula in hand.

"Only if you're offering to bring it to me!" It's not true. I'm hungry enough that I'd walk the ten steps over to the food, but if he's willing to deliver, I'll play princess.

"Would her majesty like ketchup?" Zeb asks as he approaches with a plate in one hand, ketchup bottle in the other.

"Yes, please," I say with a grin. "Thanks, dude."

"No problem, you deserve it after you girls kicked ass today on the track."

I gesture to the growing crowd on the deck. "Who are all these people?"

Zeb shrugs. "People," he answers simply. "Guess we're having a party tonight."

Well, at least I've got a comfy spot to take it all in. I'm digging into my first bite of burger when I see him. And it doesn't take long before his green eyes find me. I know immediately that he's here for me. Otherwise, he wouldn't have come to the yellow house for a track party, where I might be. As far as I can tell, he's taken great pains to avoid me, and his presence here tonight tells me he wants to talk to me. He has something to say, and he'd rather do it in this environment than alone somewhere.

My body reacts as he makes his way across the lawn, getting closer with each step. My skin is hot and tingly and I'm disappointed I *still* can't prevent my reaction to him. After everything, my body betrays me. Angrily, I take another bite of my burger and chew with aggression in an effort to defy the warmth in my belly that spreads through my limbs.

He's standing over me now, and he looks huger than ever. Only ever seeing him at a distance, I hadn't realized how much bigger his muscles had gotten. Is it possible he's grown taller too? Determined not to let him dictate the conversation, I speak first.

"Are you taller?" I ask, proud that my voice doesn't show how much he's affecting me.

He sits on the edge of a lawn chair beside me before answering. "Not recently. I grew an inch after high school but I'm done now."

I nod. "What do you want?" I ask with a mixture of genuine curiosity and hostility.

He peers at me like he's trying to figure out what's going on in my head and my heart all at once. Since I'm not even sure myself, I doubt he'll figure it out.

"You don't need me anymore, do you?" he asks quietly.

My eyes widen. "What kind of question is that?"

Jace offers a sad smile, one I'm not sure I've ever seen on him before. It makes my chest ache. "You never really needed me, Pepper," he says with some pride, I think, but also tinged with regret and sorrow.

He's wrong. Isn't he?

I've always needed him. As my best friend, family, next-door neighbor, and, once upon a time, my boyfriend. Though his most recent title was boyfriend, that's the one that seems farthest away, the most distant from us now. It's the sixteen years we had before our first kiss that is at the forefront of my mind when it comes to the word "need" and Jace Wilder. And that startles me.

"What do you want me to say, Jace? Do you want me to argue with you? I think you made it pretty clear you just wanted me to go away, like I never existed in the first place."

Jace shakes his head, like he's trying to ward off memories or thoughts. And then he sighs deeply. "I know that words won't be enough, but I owe you an apology. I'm sorry, Pepper. So fucking sorry."

"You have got to be kidding me," I mumble. "You're right, Jace, words don't mean much, coming from you."

His stricken expression, full of anguish, prevents me from continuing. He's acted like the ultimate asshole, yet I still *see* him. With some distance from my own heartbreak it makes it hard to see him as simply the asshole ex-boyfriend he was. It might be easier if that's all he was, but he was so much more than that.

"You don't wear the bracelet anymore," he comments. "Did you lose it?"

"No, and you really think I'm going to wear the bracelet?" I ask, amazed by his audacity. He made out with Madeline Brescoll in front of me, for goodness sake.

"I guess I hoped you'd have more faith in me."

I sit up now, unable to take any more of his messing with my head. "What? You gave that bracelet to me as some sort of test? When I took it off it meant I gave up on you? You didn't even give me a chance to give up on you, Jace. I had no choice in any of this so stop acting like I have one now."

He leans back abruptly, as if accepting a blow. And I stand up, leaving behind my half-eaten burger. And Jace.

He's right. I don't need him anymore, and maybe I never did.

As I walk through the house, I'm empowered by the knowledge that happiness is attainable without Jace Wilder in my life.

When someone pinches my ass as I pass through the kitchen, I yelp and swing around to find Trish grinning at me. "You walked right past me, girl. What's got you so oblivious?"

"You felt you had to assault me to get my attention?" I tease, ignoring her question.

I notice Lexi is in the kitchen too, sitting on the counter, while Brax stands between her legs. They've been glued at the hip for weeks now, apparently trying to be together "for real" this time. Seems to be working so far.

A small piece of me craves that intimacy again, but I ignore the longing, and offer to help chop onions for Trish's guacamole. Still, I can't help but wonder if one day I'll have a new boyfriend, just like I have my new friends. My college teammates and I have become closer than I ever imagined. They aren't better or more important than my Brockton friends, but somewhere along the way, they became permanent structures in my life. It's crazy that I hardly knew these girls less than a year ago. It's even crazier that someone I thought would always be in my life is probably lost to me forever.

I wonder what my happily-ever-after looks like now. If this is it – running my heart out every day with my teammates and laughing, dancing, and eating with them afterward – it's one I can embrace without regrets.

ALSO BY ALI DEAN

Pepper Jones Series

Pepped Up (Pepper Jones #1)

All Pepped Up (Pepper Jones #2)

Pepped Up & Ready (Pepper Jones #3)

Pep Talks (Pepper Jones #4)

Pepped Up Forever (Pepper Jones #5)

Pepped Up & Wilder (Pepper Jones #6)

Stark Springs Academy Series

Black Diamond

Double Black

Black Ice

Spark Sisters Series

The Line Below

Kick

Standalones

Elusive

Doubles Love

Made in the USA
Coppell, TX
18 January 2020